"I only

"Why?" she had to ask.

"When it comes to the heart, there's very little rhyme or reason." He pulled her to him. Aimee felt his power, his darkness—as blinding as love's bright light—draw her in.

She kissed him, this man so sure she would be scared or seduced. She was both, her play for power ending as soon as his lips touched hers. All rules were broken. Motives left, leaving only need.

Her body pressed against his, alive and unashamed with desire. Her mouth opened wider, hungry. She could taste his strength and power, the hot demand of his body.

She pulled away in one last grasp for control. Even in a marriage of convenience, Colin would never stand for shallow embraces, shadow kisses. He would demand nothing less than everything. He would take whatever he wanted until his bought bride would either love him or hate him...but she would be his.

Dear Reader,

When winter weather keeps you indoors, what better way to pass the time than curling up with Harlequin American Romance? Warm yourself from the inside out with our very special love stories!

There's something appealing about a big, strong man learning to care for a small child, and Linda Cajio's hero in *Family to Be*, the first book in our brand-new miniseries THE DADDY CLUB, is no exception. Ross Steadwell started The Daddy Club to help other single fathers like him—come see what happens when a woman gets in on the fun!

And what's a man to do when the woman of his dreams gets amnesia—and doesn't remember that he's the father of her child? In Charlotte Maclay's *A Daddy for Becky*, Ben Miller has an innovative answer! And up-and-coming author Darlene Scalera is not to be missed with her tale of a million-dollar marriage offer in *Man in a Million*.

Finally, Debbi Rawlins has concocted a whimsical tale of two sisters who trade places for a week and fall in love with men they wouldn't otherwise have met. *His, Hers and Theirs* offers two special heroines, two sexy heroes, two heartwarming love stories—all in one book!

A whole new year is just beginning—start it off right by treating yourself to our four newest American Romance novels!

Happy New Year!

Melissa Jeglinski
Associate Senior Editor

Man in a Million

DARLENE SCALERA

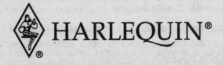

HARLEQUIN®

TORONTO • NEW YORK • LONDON
AMSTERDAM • PARIS • SYDNEY • HAMBURG
STOCKHOLM • ATHENS • TOKYO • MILAN • MADRID
PRAGUE • WARSAW • BUDAPEST • AUCKLAND

To Damaris and Denise for being the first to say yes.

ACKNOWLEDGMENT:
Special thanks and a wish of fair winds to Doug Logan
of *Sailing World*.

ISBN 0-373-16807-1

MAN IN A MILLION

Copyright © 1999 by Darlene Scalera.

This edition published by arrangement with Harlequin Books S.A.

Visit us at www.romance.net

Printed in U.S.A.

ABOUT THE AUTHOR

Darlene Scalera is a native New Yorker who graduated magna cum laude from Syracuse University with a degree in public communications. She worked in a variety of fields, including telecommunications and public relations, before devoting herself full-time to romance fiction writing. She was instrumental in forming the Saratoga, New York, chapter of Romance Writers of America and is a frequent speaker on romance writing at local schools, libraries, writing groups and women's organizations. She currently lives happily ever after in upstate New York with her husband, Jim, and their two children, J.J. and Ariana. You can write to Darlene at P.O. Box 217, Niverville, NY 12130.

Books by Darlene Scalera

HARLEQUIN AMERICAN ROMANCE

762—A MAN FOR MEGAN
807—MAN IN A MILLION

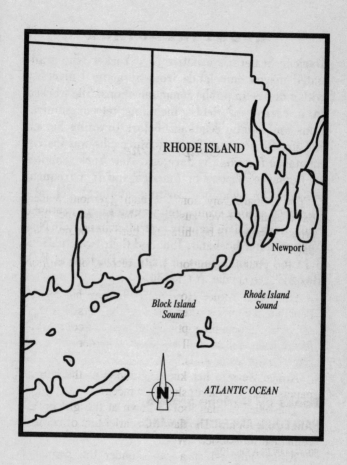

RHODE ISLAND

Newport

Rhode Island
Sound

Block Island
Sound

ATLANTIC OCEAN

Chapter One

"You'll marry my son." Vivian Tremont leaned back against velvet cushions. She folded her thin arms. "There will be children. There will be no scandals.

"For your cooperation, you'll receive one million dollars."

The folder Aimee Rose held fell from her hands. Penciled sketches scattered across the Persian rug.

"There'll be a prenuptial agreement, of course, but the million dollars will be yours whether the marriage continues or ends."

Aimee went to her knees, grabbed at the strewn papers. She felt the flush in her face.

The older woman looked down at the girl on all fours beneath her. The flawless scarlet line of her lips remained immobile. "Well?"

Aimee grabbed at a paper under the woman's chair. It was a sketch of the silk jacquard she had designed for Mrs. Van Wie last season. Nearby was the drawing of the red georgette. She shoved the papers into the folder and stared at the cardboard's sallow color. There was the sound of her uneven breaths, the light *tap tap tap* of Mrs. Tremont's fingernails as they drummed against the mahogany chair arm. Aimee sat back on her heels, pressing the sketches to her chest.

"Mrs. Tremont—"

"Call me Vivian." The woman's lips pulled back into a smile, baring even, white teeth.

"Vivian," Aimee obediently began again, "I don't understand...." Her voice faltered beneath the woman's stare. She pushed herself back up on the settee.

The woman was still smiling. Her eyes were dead-cod cold. "It's simple, my dear."

"Mrs. Tremont—Vivian," Aimee amended at the woman's sharp glance. She fingered the edge of the folder. "Do you know what you're asking me to do? You're asking me—"

"I know exactly what I'm offering you." The woman's smile dissolved. Her hands tightened on the chair arms. She leaned forward. "I'm giving you a once-in-a-lifetime opportunity."

She sat back stiffly as if forcing herself to relax. The cold-eyed smile returned. "I'll admit my proposal is a little unusual. But years ago, prearranged marriages were de rigueur. In this day of disease and divorce, there's something almost refreshingly sensible about having your mate carefully chosen for you. Think of the money as a dowry. In these liberated times, what does it matter if the bride or the groom provides it?"

Aimee looked at the woman across from her. Was this woman giving Aimee her son as calmly as she had offered a tray of tiny toast wedges moments ago?

"You see, it's simple," Vivian insisted.

Aimee could think of several adjectives to describe the proposal. *Simple* was not even on the list.

"There'll also be the standard blood tests, but, providing they're negative, there should be no problem," Vivian continued as if Aimee had already accepted the offer.

"You're afraid of disease?" Aimee was trying to understand. "That's the reason for an arranged marriage?"

"Everyone's afraid of disease," the woman replied. "But no, that isn't the reason for the arranged marriage."

Aimee waited for her to go on. She didn't.

Aimee attempted another tactic. "Your son agrees with this arrangement?"

Vivian interlaced her fingers and settled them in her lap. "My son asked me to assist him with this arrangement. I chose you."

Aimee shifted in her seat, suffering the woman's relentless gaze. "Why?" she blurted.

Vivian tilted her head back, regarding Aimee with a shrewd stare. "My dear, you underestimate yourself. You're stunning."

Her pupils contracted into black pinpoints. "And if you accept my offer, you'll not only be beautiful… you'll be rich."

Aimee shook her head. "I still don't understand—"

"Don't trouble yourself with the details. Just know this—if you say yes to my proposal, your life will never be the same."

Vivian stood up, indicating the meeting was over.

"Of course, I don't expect an answer today. I realize this is a little more complicated than choosing fried clams or lobster roll for lunch." Her lips twisted in an imitation of a smile.

Aimee stood up, still shaking her head. "I really don't think—"

"That's right. Don't think right now." Vivian's hand clutched Aimee's forearm as she guided her out to the paneled hall. "I understand you'll need time to consider my offer. After all," she added with a brittle laugh, "it's not every day a girl gets a marriage proposal."

Aimee gave a sideways glance of disbelief. *Marriage proposal* was a polite way of putting what had just been suggested. And Vivian knew it. Aimee looked down. The older woman's manicured fingernails were imprinted ruby against her pale flesh.

"I'll be in touch." Vivian dismissed her as they reached the foyer.

The solid oak door closed behind Aimee with a loud thud. She hurried down the marble steps, pausing at the bottom to catch her breath. Beyond the sloping lawn, the Atlantic Ocean surged, then retreated, rolling back with an endless shudder. Aimee looked back at the mansion. Her gaze fluttered to the second story. A dark silhouette was framed in a tall window. Aimee turned around, meeting the vast power of the sea. With quick steps, she hurried away from the house.

COLIN TREMONT STARED out at the ocean. Large, heavy waves rolled into the shore. Voices from beyond the bedroom rose and fell. Words rushed out in anger. The waves broke against the rocks. Colin heard his half brother speak in the hall, his voice swelled with indignation:

"The old man is mad."

Shawn's mother answered, "Mad or not, he owns the company's controlling interest. The houses, the stocks, all other assets are in his name. He has the power to carry out this plan."

"I won't be threatened," Shawn said.

"Make no mistake," Vivian warned her son. "Hugo isn't threatening. The lawyers have been called in, and the will is already in the process of being rewritten. All of Hugo's fortune will go to the grandson who marries first."

"I'm the entitled heir."

"Hugo's finished with your frivolous life-style," Vivian said shortly. "He wants you to take seriously the responsibility of being a Tremont."

The voices began to fade as mother and son moved down the hall.

"I won't do it," Shawn said.

Vivian's voice was fainter, but its sharp ruthlessness still carried. "You'll do exactly as is asked. I endured too much to guarantee you everything, and I'm not about to give it all up to your father's bastard son."

Colin stepped back from the window, releasing the heavy brocade curtain, relinquishing the image of the beautiful girl below. The bedroom was bathed once again in shadows.

A chaise lounge was situated in the corner. Colin ignored its long, inviting curves and sat on its narrow end. So, his grandfather had decided it was time for his grandsons to marry. That was why Colin had been summoned from New York a week before scheduled.

Would he do it? At his side, Colin's fist clenched and unclenched like a heart beating. The question was moot. He'd spent his whole life trying to make up for the scandal which had resulted in the unfortunate occurrence of his birth. He'd achieved an impeccable record at prep school, graduated top of his class from Harvard, then took his place at the helm of Seventh Avenue and West Seventeenth Street, home of Leonard's of New York where the Tremont retailing empire humbly began four generations earlier. Being a Tremont was all he'd ever known.

Colin stood up. The answer had been decided long before his grandfather would call him down to the darkly paneled library and set forth his terms over a civil snifter of hundred-year-old cognac. The answer had been decided a generation earlier, when a beautiful fortune hunter had seduced Colin's father, Hugo's first and only born, and almost destroyed this family. Now Colin would have to find another gorgeous gold digger to save it.

He walked again to the window. The wind had picked up, causing the waves to rise, jabbing and punching at the sky. Gray, rain-soaked clouds shrouded the sun. The weather was changing.

AIMEE'S BROTHER, JACK, put down his glass. A thin mustache of milk coated his upper lip. ''She couldn't have been serious.'' With the back of his hand, he wiped his mouth.

His sister carried her glass of milk and plate of

boiled macaroni and cheese to the table. "Obviously you've never met Vivian Tremont."

"We don't exactly run in the same circles."

"Believe me, the woman was serious. She's not the practical-joker type."

Jack stood and refilled his plate from a pot on the stove. Leaning against the counter, he speared a forkful of noodles. "So when's the wedding?"

Aimee felt her face turn hot. "I'd never marry for money, Jack. You know that."

"Easy, little sis. I was kidding."

"Well, don't even kid about something like that. When I marry, it'll be for love—not money."

"Is that what you told Vivian Tremont?"

The color beginning to subside in Aimee's cheeks flared again. "Not exactly."

Jack's eyebrows lifted. "Not exactly?" he said through a mouthful of bright orange noodles.

"I tried to…" Aimee pushed the macaroni on her plate around with a fork. "She's a very intimidating woman."

"She can afford to be."

"I can't believe I thought she'd heard about those outfits I designed for the boutique and wanted to discuss them with me. I even brought a few sketches with me. I thought, if Vivian Tremont, the grande dame of Newport's summer society, wears one of my designs…"

Her voice faltered. She busied herself sprinkling salt over her macaroni. "She must've thought I'd just fallen off the turnip truck."

Jack scraped his plate and stuck his dishes in the

sink. "If she'd taken a minute to look at your designs, she wouldn't have thought so."

Aimee smiled affectionately at her brother. "Now we both know Vivian Tremont has closets full of personally-designed Saint Laurent, Valentino, and Givenchy outfits. Why would she be impressed with the sketches of a shop clerk?"

"Because you've got talent. My customers loved the outfits you made for them last year."

"It was only two women, Jack. Two very nice, old women who've been good customers of yours since you started the business. You know old lady Carnes gets dressed each afternoon and sits in the garden, talking to the sculptures as though she were holding high tea. And last summer, didn't Lily Prescott put her Bentley in reverse and almost run you over when you were trimming the shrubs?"

"Just because they're crazy doesn't mean they don't have good taste," Jack pointed out.

Aimee allowed a smile before her expression turned serious. "Do these people think just because they have more money than Fort Knox, they can buy people?"

"Yup." Her brother took a final swig of his milk. "They do it every day. It's a matter of economics— they who have the purse, hold the power."

Aimee pushed her plate away. "That gives them the right to think they can own me?"

"I hate to tell you this, little sis, but they already do. The rich own you, me, and every other working-class stiff in this country. Look around you. There's the cottages on Bellevue Avenue. Downtown, the big-time developers are building faster than you can say time-share, and the Tremonts themselves are financing the new megamall on the waterfront. Face it, sis, we need our millionaires. They don't need us.''

Aimee looked at her brother. ''I thought we came here to get away from a world where people do things for money.''

Jack squatted down in front of her and took her hands in his. ''I don't know if such a place exists.''

Up close, she saw the dark circles of fatigue beneath his eyes. She felt the calluses padding his palms. He was working seven days a week, twelve to fourteen hours a day.

''That new lawn-care franchise is cutting your prices, isn't it?''

''Everything's fine,'' he said. ''Things have been much worse than this.''

Even this vague reference to their past brought pain into her brother's features. Then, the curtain dropped across his expression, forbidding further thought of their childhood. Still, Aimee saw her mother, dressing, preparing to go out to meet her ''gentlemen'' customers. Nana, tight-lipped, would be in the front room, ironing the silk undies of wealthy women, wives whose husbands would meet Aimee's mother that evening or another.

When her brother tried to release her hands, Aimee held fast. ''We're not whores, Jack. It's not hereditary.''

Jack's hands tightened so hard on hers, it hurt, but she showed no pain. ''That was a long, long time ago,'' he told her. ''It's over now. We've got each other. We'll get by.''

She looked into the face of her brother, mother, father, friend. She saw no further sign of the pain, so carefully denied, yet carried deep within their hearts. "We always do," she said softly.

He relaxed his grip on her hands. "You tell Vivian Tremont to save her millions. She's going to need them when she fills her closets with your fancy dresses. I've got to get to work."

As soon as Aimee arrived at the boutique the next morning, Mrs. Demers, the owner's mother, motioned her over to where she was standing, phone in one hand. She covered the mouthpiece with her other hand. "It's Mrs. Tremont again," she told Aimee in a reverent whisper. "And she wants to speak to you." She held out the receiver as if handing Aimee the Holy Grail.

"Aimee." Vivian's well-enunciated voice came over the wire. "I'm having a little party tonight. Around eight. Formal attire. Forgive the last-minute invitation, but I'm certain you can come."

"Mrs. Tremont—"

"Vivian, Vivian, Vivian," came back the musical scolding.

"Vivian, I'm glad you called—"

"I'm glad I did, too." the other woman overrode Aimee's refusal before it'd even formed into words. "I'll see you this evening." The line went dead.

Aimee stared down into the small holes of the receiver until the dial tone started to beep. She set down the phone. Mrs. Demers pretended to be busy dusting off the glass case nearby, but she'd obviously heard what little of the conversation Aimee had been able to inject. The older woman looked up with a hint of a smile and burning curiosity in her squinty eyes.

Aimee smiled back uncertainly. "Well, it looks like Cinderella is going to the ball."

SHE PAUSED in the room's doorway. Crystal chandeliers shimmered above, making the darkness outside the tall windows seem even blacker. The men and women met, then parted, forming a swirling kaleidoscope across the polished floor. There was music and the sound of laughter amid the murmur of silk and chiffon. A couple floated by, the woman inadvertently bumping Aimee. "I'm so sorry," she gushed, the jewels in her ears catching the light above.

"No problaimo," Aimee assured her, wincing even as the words rushed from her mouth. The woman's smooth face allowed a half smile before she continued on, taking delicate steps in her slim skirt.

Aimee ran her hands down the sides of her dress. She shouldn't have come, but Jack had talked her into it, insisting she could make important customer contacts. He'd even picked out her dress and threatened to embroider *Designed by Aimee* across her backside as he pushed her out the door.

She spotted Vivian in the center of the room and automatically took a step toward her. Then she stopped. As if sensing Aimee's distress, Vivian turned and came toward her.

At the other end of the room, Colin crossed his arms and leaned against the wall, watching the hesitant movements of the slender blonde sheathed in white, recognizing her as the girl he'd seen from the bedroom window yesterday. Even now, across the room, he sensed her fear. His mouth twisted in a dry smile as he watched Vivian approach her and guide her to the center of the crowded room. *Like a lamb being led to slaughter,* he thought.

Vivian handed Aimee a stemmed glass. "Here's to new friends," she toasted. "Aimee, may I present Mrs. C. D. Duke and..."

Aimee took a sip of champagne. Vivian continued to introduce the tight circle of people. The names were already familiar to Aimee but, until now, the faces had only been seen in grainy newsprint or glimpsed from behind the smooth rise of a tinted limousine window. When the presentations were finished, the hostess raised her drink, but her glass stopped midair. Her gaze went past Aimee's bare shoulder. A pleased smile lifted her lips.

"Aimee, I'd like you to meet my son...."

Aimee turned. The shy smile that had begun to charm her lips trembled, then dissolved beneath a gaze arrogant and bold with sensuality. She stared wordlessly into eyes black as the night beyond the windows. Heavy black eyebrows arched with amusement.

She had seen enough pictures of Vivian's golden-haired son, Shawn, in the society pages to anticipate a man of classical good looks tempered by an amiable smile. The complete opposite stood before her.

"Colin Tremont." Vivian completed the introduction.

The man spared a mocking acknowledgment to

Vivian, then his gaze, now cool and assessing, moved back to Aimee.

She stepped back. The hand she had started to extend stopped.

"You're Vivian's son?" It was no more than a whisper.

He took her hesitant hand. Cold fingers wrapped around her palm. "Vivian's slip of maternal instinct stems from her distaste for the more vulgar connotation of *half brother, half-breed, black sheep....*" He granted Vivian another mocking glance. "Should I continue?"

"No." Vivian was smiling, the word coming out through clamped teeth. "I believe you've made your position clear to everyone here."

Aimee had heard of him, bits and pieces of talk idly bantered in the store, around town but, until now, he'd been a stranger to Newport's summer society. *Women's Wear Daily* had called him the Tyrant of Seventh Avenue. His friends said he was a brilliant businessman. His enemies said he was born a bastard and did everything he could to live up to the title.

If she'd ever seen a picture of him, she knew she'd have remembered it. Even though she doubted a photo could do justice to the reality before her.

His dark, hooded eyes demanded she look now, as if knowing the curiosity that followed him wherever he went. His nose was too large; his black hair too long, curling against the white collar of his evening shirt. His lips were generous and born in an insolent curve. It was a face women feared...a face revered...a face remembered.

"Colin." Vivian broke the spell. "Could you practice your social skills on Aimee for a few minutes while I check on the kitchen?"

The glancing look Colin sent Vivian this time was mildly intrigued.

She laid a jeweled hand on his arm. "Be gentle with her, darling."

Colin turned a sudden smile to Aimee, but his features smoothed, denying scrutiny. His eyes never leaving her face, he removed the empty glass from her hand and exchanged it for a full one from a passing tray.

She managed to take the slender glass with a slight smile of thanks. She refused his offer of food with a mute shake of her head. Clever conversation was beyond her shaken sensibilities at the moment. She turned her attention to the dancers.

She chanced a sidelong glance at the dark profile beside her. Which Tremont son wanted to buy a bride?

"Would you like to dance?" Colin asked.

The image of her dancing with this man came as if he'd already taken her hand, wrapped his arm around her waist and pressed her to his chest.

She found her voice. "Perhaps later?"

He nodded. "As you wish."

Couples danced, meeting and parting in a relief of rich colors and glittering gems. It was all a blinding blur to Aimee, her senses held hostage by the man beside her. His almost-touching nearness was worse than if she had allowed him to hold her close among the couples on the floor with his hand on the dip of her spine, the strength of his muscles felt through the fine material of his shirt. He merely stood nearby, not touching her, not looking at her. She could barely hear him breathing. Yet every inch of her body was being branded.

"If you don't mind, I'd really like to sit down."

He led her to a row of high-backed chairs against the wall. He waited, watching her, as she sat down on the edge of a red velvet cushion.

She thanked him once more. "I've been on my feet all day. I'm a working girl. Tonight I'm just seeing how the other half lives."

He smiled down at her. "And you find it to your liking?"

Aimee looked up into the dangerous depths of those eyes. Was this the son who wanted a wife? she wondered. She looked at those mesmerizing features and saw the edge of ruthlessness.

If he was the one, how much had Vivian told him about her? She didn't want him to think she was even considering the insulting offer. But first she had to determine if he was the one who wished to buy his bride.

"Actually, I don't really know what I'm doing here. I had a meeting with Vivian yesterday and…" She waited for his reaction, hoping for a clue.

The brazen smile loomed above her. "A business meeting? Or something of a more personal nature?"

Aimee pleated the white crepe of her skirt. "A little bit of both."

His words had told her nothing; his expression even less. If he did know about the offer, he would know she hadn't refused it yet.

"I assume the meeting was satisfactory to both parties?" he asked.

She looked up into those eyes and saw fine lines of amusement at their corners. She still didn't know if he was the son seeking a bride, but, in case he was, she had to attempt to explain her current falsely compromised position.

"I learned Vivian doesn't take no for an answer."

He threw back his head, and she didn't think he could laugh so full and long and with such pure pagan joy. She felt it incense her even as it drew her to him. Others stared.

He leaned in too close to her. She could feel the nakedness of her shoulders, the swell of her breasts against the tight dip of her neckline.

"Neither do I, darling." His gaze lingered, scoring the span of her exposed skin. Finally he straightened, his gaze releasing her.

She nervously raised her glass to her lips. When had it become empty?

"Let me get you another."

"Why not?" She tried to make her laugh as light as the cut crystal flute she held up to him. She had the uneasy sensation they'd already begun that dance he'd earlier offered. Her laugh spilled sharp and tight, and she felt dizzy from the vintage champagne, the chandeliers' too-soft light, the man all shadows and darkness above her.

He looked down at her for a final moment, then left. She watched him thread his way through the crowd, ignoring the others. She saw the smooth power of muscle, the rippling strength of ligament, the proud thrust of his head. He moved like a silent scourge through the room. Even from a distance, Aimee was frightened...and fascinated.

So intent was her study of the man, she didn't realize someone else had approached her chair until she heard, "It's a rare woman who can make my half brother laugh."

She looked up into a shiny surface of bronzed handsomeness. Warm white-blue eyes looked down at her above a wide, white smile. For Aimee, no introductions were necessary.

Still, the man bent low and kissed her hand without her permission and announced "Shawn Tremont." The aqua eyes were translucent as shallow pools. The smile too perfect. Here, standing above Aimee, was the creature made for a marriage of convenience.

"Aimee Rose." She answered the waiting question in his eyes.

"Aimee Rose." He tasted the name. His fingers tightened on hers for a moment, but she felt no fear. In the fair face above her was no threat, no depth, only the placidness of perfection. After the storm that was Colin, this man was the surface calm.

How could she have mistaken Colin for the man who wanted to buy a bride? It was obvious Shawn was the man who could thrive in a marriage of convenience, breezing through life on a ship of golden smiles, a properly chosen companion at his side.

She smiled almost sympathetically at the man whose surface was as thin and glossy as the magazine pages he was so often pictured on. She was certain Shawn would never demand more than a well-groomed, well-connected wife, beautiful, blue-eyed heirs and an endless cycle of social engagements.

Colin would demand more. Unbidden into her thoughts came Colin's face, resplendent in its savage masculinity, unrepentant in its wanton sensuality.

Colin would demand everything.

Two brothers, day and night, one as dark as the other was light. Aimee's thoughts were a child's rhyme, an ageless riddle. One wanted to buy a wife, and why? the riddle continued.

And why had she been chosen? Why had she, a working-class shop clerk who'd begun her life as the daughter of a Providence harbor whore, been offered the son of Newport's wealthiest family?

Chapter Two

"I see you've managed to amuse yourself in my absence."

Aimee looked up, meeting Colin's gaze. Her smile slipped away. He handed her the glass of champagne, looking at her a minute longer than necessary before he turned to his half brother.

He nodded, his jaw drawn into a sharp line. "Shawn."

"Colin," the other man acknowledged with a wink of his blue-white gaze.

Each man stood, instinctively squared off, ignoring the other. Aimee sipped her champagne. The silence grew loud.

Colin's gaze descended on her. "Would you dance with me now?"

"Sorry, little brother." Shawn's voice was silky with sarcasm. He took Aimee's hand and pulled her to her feet. "I've already been promised the next dance."

He led her away. As they took their place amid the swaying couples, she felt Colin's eyes following them. She turned into Shawn's arms, and Colin's stare met hers, impaling her with its verdict. She dropped her gaze, but not before she saw his full lips lift with amusement.

"Did you win?" she asked Shawn.

His wide, white smile was constant. "Not yet, but I will."

He only smiled at her baffled expression. His hand moved from her waist to the small of her back, inviting her closer out here under the diffused light, steering her farther from the dark unknown that was Colin.

Yet she was conscious of the other man. From the corner of her eye, she could see him watching her, the firm set of his mouth passing judgment. She threw back her head, exposing the smooth white cord of her neck. Her lips smiled. Her eyes focused on Shawn, but they spoke to Colin. *Be damned,* they said.

COLIN WATCHED the couple—both beautiful, blond. He watched Aimee lift her flawless face toward Shawn, her pale blue eyes mirrored in his. He watched her smile at something Shawn whispered in her ear. A pang of jealousy erupted from somewhere previously undisturbed. He refused to oblige it. *Leave it to Vivian,* he thought, *to find the perfect sacrificial virgin.*

"ARE YOU QUESTIONING my motives to dance with a beautiful girl?" Shawn asked Aimee, his eyes asking more.

She resisted the coaxing pressure on her spine. Shawn's attentions were well honed, designed to make her feel as light as the champagne bubbles she could still taste. Yet, like those bubbles rising delicately, then burst, she knew his attentions were equally ephemeral. In that everlasting smile and those easy compliments, it was simple to see he only desired women to flock to him, to admire him like the crowds that gather round a rarity. Shawn drew women to him like bees to honey.

Colin captured them like a spider spinning a web.

"You and your brother are so different," she said.

Shawn gave a soundless laugh and whirled her to the right. The chandelier sprinkled diamonds of light across his face, highlighting the perfection of his features. Only Aimee, so close, could see the slight cloud in the clear blue of his eyes.

"Colin is my half brother," he corrected.

"Half brother?" Aimee echoed what she already knew, but she wanted to know more.

Shawn nodded. "Same father, different mothers. Vivian is my mother. Colin's mother was some Broadway half hoofer, half hooker."

Aimee pulled back.

"Excuse my crudeness." He attributed the sudden space between them. With a practiced hand, he brought her close once more. "While he was married to my mother, my father thought he'd found true love on the Great White Way. He and the Broadway babe were on their way to a weekend rendezvous when the private jet went down. Colin had been left with one of the other girls in the chorus. The family found out about him when she dumped him, four months old, in my grandfather's lap at the memorial service, demanding money or sure scandal. Nearly killed the old man. Hell, nearly felled the whole Tremont family tree.'' Shawn's pausing laugh was quick and caustic.

''Hugo paid up, but the hush money couldn't guarantee complete silence—only whispers. Shh.'' Shawn put a finger to his lips and dropped his lids low. ''If you listen closely, you'll hear them even now.''

Aimee couldn't help glance right and left. The story seemed to surround her like the shadows dodging and dipping in the room's muted light. Her eyes looked for Colin and found him, the orphaned child.

''And so Hugo bought Colin into the family as if the bastard belonged here. Enough about Colin,'' Shawn said closing the subject. The smile returned automatically.

''He's probably bored you to tears already with tales of Seventh Avenue year-end earnings and proposed joint ventures, and now I'm guilty of the same-old, same-old, too.''

''Believe me,'' Aimee said, ''tonight has been anything but boring.''

''Just because you're Colin's date, doesn't mean you have to defend him. His idea of a wild time is watching old videotapes of *Wall Street in Review*.''

''I'm not Colin's date.'' Aimee had stiffened in Shawn's arms.

''C'mon. Your secret's safe with me.''

This was the son who wanted to buy a wife, Aimee's thoughts insisted. He should know all about Vivian's offer.

Then why did he assume she was Colin's date?

''It was your mother who invited me here this evening.'' She fished, watching for his response. ''She insisted. She wouldn't take no for an answer.''

Shawn smiled his beguiling smile. His aqua eyes assessed her. ''Mother.'' He shook his fair head. ''She never got over my father's betrayal. Since then, she's determined not to let things get beyond her control.''

Aimee stepped back. ''Some things are beyond her control.''

Shawn never stopped smiling. ''But you're here, aren't you?''

She couldn't deny it. The music ended without answers.

She pulled away, anxious to leave, to put sudden distance between herself and this large house full of small secrets.

''Thank you, but I've got to go,'' she murmured, and turned to leave before Shawn could even express a polite protest. She blended in between the other couples coming off the dance floor and headed toward the door. In her haste, she didn't see the elderly gentleman with a cane until they collided.

''Oh, good gosh.'' She grasped at the man's arm to steady him. ''I'm so sorry. I didn't see you.''

''No harm done, my dear. Vivian insists on following the Newport unwritten rule of overcrowding all affairs.'' Eyes faded blue smiled at her. The man pointed his cane at the chairs. ''But if you'd be kind enough to assist me…''

''Certainly.'' Aimee took his arm.

''Truthfully,'' the elderly gentleman confided as they began to walk toward the other side of the room,

"I want my grandsons to see me walking with the prettiest girl here."

She smiled. They were almost to the chairs when she saw Colin approaching them. Shawn was behind him. The smile left her face.

"See." The old man looked at her with eyes dimmed with age and winked. "I told you we'd get their attention."

"Hugo," Colin said, his gaze alighting on Aimee before settling on his grandfather. "Are you okay?"

The patriarch of the Tremont family selected a chair and sat, ignoring both Colin and Shawn's outstretched hands of assistance.

"If either one of you," he spoke to his grandsons, "had the common sense God gave you, you'd be worrying about why this lovely girl was all alone, instead of fussing over an old fool like me. But no." He lifted his cane and pointed it at the offending parties.

"One—" he steered his cane slowly to Shawn "—plays like the devil. The other—" the cane came Colin's way "—works like a fiend."

Shawn's smile faded, his face almost becoming mortal. Colin's expression betrayed nothing.

"Since we've determined you're in no immediate danger," Shawn said to Hugo, "and I've duly received my daily comeuppance, I'll be off."

Colin stayed, standing to the left of Aimee, his presence as tangible as the night wind slipping in through the nearby garden doors.

Hugo patted the seat next to him. "Please sit down, my dear," he said to her, "and we'll give all the others something to speculate about."

"Actually, I was on my way out," she explained, conscious of Colin's study.

"Seen enough?" he asked her.

She turned to him. His expression was smooth, closed.

"It's been a long time since I've had the freshest flower in the room at my side," Hugo said. "Please sit down and tell me about yourself, my dear."

"Aimee's a working girl," Colin said behind her.

She shot him a sharp glance, but before she could respond, Vivian swept down upon the trio. Her gaze made a critical circle from Hugo to Aimee to Colin. She smiled the artful smile of a hostess. "Aimee, I see you've met all of the Tremont men."

"Vivian, where did you dig up this little gal?" Hugo asked.

"Yes, Vivian," Colin echoed. "Where did you dig up this little gal?"

Vivian smiled, showing her teeth. "I interviewed her only yesterday about coming to work for me."

"In what capacity?" Amusement laced the lazy pace of Colin's words.

Vivian turned to him. More white teeth showed. "I need someone to help me out with my plans for the summer season. I haven't given the position an official title yet."

"How about *lady-in-waiting?*" Colin suggested.

Aimee had heard enough. "Actually, I enjoy my present job at The Dressing Room." She interrupted the discussion, indignation churning within her. "One day I'll be selling my own designs from my own boutique, so it's great experience. I'm learning the business from the bottom up."

"The bottom, yes," Vivian noted with a light laugh. "Isn't she delightful, Hugo?"

"That's where it all begins—at the bottom. At the turn of the century, my great-grandfather, Leonard Tremont, hocked his wife's engagement ring for two hundred dollars and used the money to buy forty men's suits and pay one month's rent on a little storefront in Manhattan's Chelsea section. And here we are today—" the old man looked around the room "—reaping the rewards."

His gaze fell on Shawn across the room. His grandson was leaning against the bar, his collar loosened, a glass of champagne in each hand and a woman next to him, her head close to receive his whispers.

"Some of us are masters at reaping the rewards," Hugo commented.

"Edmund Fitzpatrick is waiting for you in the library, Hugo." Vivian turned the old man's attention away from Shawn.

"Yes." Hugo leaned on his cane to rise. Colin's hand grasped his elbow. Vivian came around to the old man's other side and tried to link her arm through his.

"I'm fine, thank you." Hugo brushed away the helping hands. Throwing his weight on the golden head of his cane, he straightened. When he looked down at Aimee, he smiled, but his eyes belied the effect of his efforts.

"Thank you for keeping an old coot company. I hope we'll have another chance to have our conversation."

"Of course you will." Vivian said. Aimee felt the

weight of her gaze. "This is only the first night of many. Shall we go?" She spoke to Hugo, but her eyes stayed on Aimee.

With his head held high, Hugo allowed his daughter-in-law to take his arm. Aimee watched the couple cross the floor with careful steps. Beyond them, she saw Shawn dance by in a whirl of black and white and gold, another girl held tightly in his arms, the constant smile on his face. Then the young couple swept away, and Hugo's shuffling form, propped up by Vivian, came back into focus.

"How sick is he?" she asked Colin as she watched the older pair.

"The doctors give him a year. But they don't come tougher than Hugo. For him, a year could mean ten."

Aimee looked up at Colin, but he was watching his grandfather. The black steel of his eyes had softened. His gaze shifted to her. His eyes became cast metal once more, deflecting her stare. She turned away, directing her focus back to the dance floor. Shawn danced by, the same smile on his face as a new girl tilted her face up to his in open rapture.

"I have to go." Aimee stood up.

As Shawn waltzed by, he winked at her over the shoulder of the petite blonde in pale pink.

"I'm sure he'll be back to rescue you soon," Colin noted.

She looked at him. "Am I in danger?" She watched his eyes. Like the ocean they were—one minute placid and calm; the next, raging, swirling with storm, all power and threat.

A smile slowly spread his lips. "Definitely." Each syllable was pronounced.

Beneath his gaze, she could feel the bareness of her shoulders, the fine feel of her dress, the edge of her skirt just touching her thigh.

"Good night." She didn't offer her hand, not wanting to risk a final touch. There was a heat inside her and around her, closing off her breath. Wide French doors leading out to the garden were only steps away. She backed away toward the twin doors and the promise of cool, clean air sent by the sea.

Colin stepped toward her. He could be taken with her; he could be toying with her. She couldn't tell. She feared he was about to stop her; she feared he wouldn't. She was caught in his sorcerer's stare.

"Next time we'll dance," he said.

She opened her mouth to protest, to insist there wouldn't be another time. When would a common shop clerk and a merchant prince meet again? Over cocktails and bacon-bit canapś at the Clambake Casino? Strolling along Bellevue Avenue in the shadows of Newport's many sixty-room "cottages"?

Yet, even as the refusal formed, she couldn't utter the words. She looked into the dark promise of Colin's eyes and knew the dance had already begun.

She stumbled out into the garden, taking great drafts of air, not looking back over her shoulder. She hurried, the night scents and sounds of the garden rising, surrounding her, the constant breath of the sea calling. She hit something hard. It was a stone bench. Her legs went weak, forcing her to stop.

She sat on cold marble beneath the disguise of

darkness. She could still see the lights of the party, hear laughter and the low, sweet coax of music.

Inside were two brothers, two sons, bound by a father whose own passion had destroyed him. One brother wanted a wife.

There was Shawn, who left a woman feeling like a child who'd eaten too much candy, suffering a sweet taste in her mouth and an emptiness in her stomach. Still, Aimee had no proof he was the son who wanted to buy a bride.

There was Colin, a chasm of dark secrets and darker feelings. Pity the poor woman who was tempted by his cool demeanor and came too close, thinking she could take his heart. For Aimee knew there would be no peace with a man like that. His desire would drown a woman; his passion would poison her. He would seduce her, then scoff at her. Aimee saw it in his eyes' scornful shine. She felt it in the seemingly benign turn of his head.

"Colin." She risked the name on her lips.

She knew fear as cold as the marble beneath her. She knew fascination as strange as the sudden soft sound of breath leaving her body. Couldn't ruthlessness be enough reason to offer cold cash for a wife?

Still, her instinct insisted it wasn't Colin. Only Shawn, all groomed charm and manners, could expect a woman to find happiness in no more than money and the perfection of her husband's face.

But Colin. Aimee felt the strangling tightness in her chest. She parted her lips farther, forcing the rose-scented air into her lungs. Even in a marriage of convenience, Colin would never stand for shallow embraces, shadow kisses. He would demand nothing less than everything. He would take whatever he wanted until his bought bride would either love him or hate him…but she would be his.

COLIN GAVE UP on sleep at dawn and went to the old workshop in the back of the carriage house. He smiled when he saw the broken chair over a century old. He'd moved most of his tools and materials when he bought the cottage on Block Island, but there were still a few unfinished pieces here. He'd begun collecting and restoring pieces of furniture while in his teens. Odds and ends unwanted, dulled, broken. Diamonds in the rough, waiting for his touch. His hands would strip, sand, stain the antique pieces, and he would know a connection, a sense of history.

His own history had been bought and paid in full at four months old. A Tremont was what he was to be—nothing less. From his efforts, the Tremont name had earned recognition; the Tremont fortune had increased.

Still, he saw the resentment in the others' eyes. In the end, he remained Hugo's only son's final sin.

He ran his hand down the chair leg, seeking the warmth of the wood beneath his palm. He felt only hardness. He reached for a rag darkened with mineral spirits.

Damn them. Clever Vivian still scheming to make someone pay for her husband's betrayal. Shawn, society's sweet prince, intent on satisfying himself and his pleasures above all else. Hugo, more than a grandfather, less than a father. Whatever little love Colin had known had come grudgingly from this man. Colin couldn't love him anything but fiercely. And as Hugo commanded, he would prove it one last time.

He polished the wood with swift, strong strokes. Damn them all. Even the girl who'd been lured into the circle, obviously cajoled by Vivian to be Shawn's bride. What had she been offered, or was she truly the ingenue she portrayed, content enough with the promise of wealth, position and a handsome, blond husband who would change partners as effortlessly as he did this evening, sending her staggering out into the night? Colin had been tempted to go after her, but then, well, she had made her own bed, hadn't she?

Still, she haunted him. His thoughts formed her name. Aimee. His hand tightened on the length of wood. He saw her even now—hair like spun sunlight snaking across a breast, shoulders bared, smooth as opals. He shook his head as if to awaken from a dream.

For this was no time for dreams. The battle had begun yesterday when Hugo had called each grandson into the darkly paneled room and told them of the change in the will. Whichever grandson married first would be rewarded sole control of the family fortune.

Shawn had sputtered and sulked. Colin had sat silent. If Shawn gained controlling interest in Leonard's, the chain would be in financial ruin before the first fiscal year was over. Colin wouldn't allow that to happen to the company or the employees who'd helped Leonard's prosper in a time when grander retailing giants had been blackened with bankruptcy.

And, so, as his grandfather wished, he would marry and father sons, strong representatives of the Tremont name.

He saw Aimee once more. He smiled now, understanding why her image had stayed uninvited in his mind. She was the answer. If she'd said yes to be Shawn's bride, with the right incentives, couldn't she be persuaded to shift her loyalties and marry him? They'd be honeymooning before Vivian could lure another victim.

The family business would continue to profit; thousands of employees' jobs would be secured; children would come to carry on the Tremont name. And he, deemed the family's shame, would become the family's savior.

Having determined his end, he must decide his means. The seesaw motion of his arm slowed. Vivian must've offered money. It was the easiest and most effective enticement. He had his generous salary and some assets, but he couldn't compete with Vivian in a bidding war.

But what if he offered wealth sweetened with something much more subtle but triple in strength? Something that turned old ladies young and grown men like his father into fools.

Would the girl see right through his ploy or was she the novice she seemed? He saw her as she had looked last evening, paused at the entrance to the gilded lions' den, her lips parted, her eyes wide and ringed with white. She had looked lost, vulnerable, so alone, something inside him had awakened, something that should have never stirred from its slumber.

But when Vivian had offered her the position of

being Mrs. Shawn Tremont, had the clear blue eyes gone glassy with greed? Had the lips spread with a serene siren's smile?

Virgin or vixen? Did it matter? For Colin knew hearts were no more than the wood he worked on now: none are so hard they can't be softened; none are so strong they can't be broken; none are so pure they can't be stained.

It was simple. He'd pretend to offer his own heart, securing hers in return.

AIMEE AWOKE EARLY the next morning and, for a moment, before full consciousness came, she remembered the ripple of silk, the rustle of satin. She saw stiff white collars and tailored seams beneath a chandelier's sweet anointment. It was her young girl's dream when, huddled in a cold corner, she'd lose herself in the lovely lines of a dress or the soft feel of fabric, sketching and sewing, dreaming of clothes that could cover bodies broken, hearts scarred.

Then Aimee remembered Vivian's offer and woke fully.

She dressed for work, but still memories whispered. She saw her nana, her arthritic hands carrying a basket of rich women's soiled laundry; she saw her mother counting her night's take, a flash of diamonds in her ears from one of her more generous customers.

Why hadn't she told Vivian ''no'' yet? she questioned herself as she walked to work. Why had she drunk her champagne, danced upon her marble floor? Was it because, deep down, she was no more than her mother's daughter?

No! The answer, the anger came on a burning intake of breath. How dare Vivian Tremont treat her like no more than a bauble seen and selected from a shop window? She walked on, taking huge swallows of the sharp sea air. She looked to her left. Her view was blocked by concrete condominiums climbing into the sky. Her anger spiraled as high. She walked past an empty storefront. The small businesses couldn't compete with the giant retailers, and they were falling like dominoes. She came to her own place of work and stopped, taking again several deep breaths. She looked all around her, seeing everywhere the unmistakable mark of big money. Helplessness rose like bile in her throat.

How dare they tempt her.

The store's back door was already opened, but she knew it was her boss's desire for fresh Danish rather than worry over a crowd of shoppers that accounted for his early arrival. On the contrary, things had been so slow lately, he'd talked about not opening on Sundays anymore. He was at the front counter now, behind the cash register. He looked up at her. He didn't smile.

"Morning, Benny." She walked toward the front.

"How'd your meeting with Vivian Tremont go?"

She stopped midstep. "About as she expected."

Benny's brow puckered. "Was she interested in your designs?"

"No, we didn't discuss my designs at all." Aimee deliberately kept her expression bland.

Benny's features, however, sank with disappointment. "Oh, I was hoping…"

She stepped closer to the man. "It's okay, Benny.

You'll just have to be stuck with my undiscovered talent.'' She smiled, hoping for one in return.

Her boss's face remained grim. "It's just that, well, Aimee, you do have a lot of talent, and you're an excellent worker. Don't you think you'd be happier at one of the newer, bigger stores planned for the new mall? Leonard's of New York is going to be the anchor store, and being you know Vivian Tremont—''

"Leave you, Benny? Not a chance. Who else would allow me to put my own designs on display? Not one of those cookie-cutter, chain stores with the too-thin mannequins in the front windows mocking every woman that walks by. Don't think I'm not happy here because—''

"Aimee, I've got to let you go," Benny blurted.

She stared at him, her mouth frozen on the words she was about to form.

"The store's closing. I can't compete with the big guns coming in from New York, Chicago and California. I hardly have enough business now to pay the monthly overhead. In the next few months, almost all of the businesses in this part of town will have closed or moved to the mall.''

"You could move to the mall," she suggested.

"The rents are too high—triple what I'm paying now, and I don't have the capital to get started again. I'm sorry.''

She shook her head. "It's not your fault.''

"Listen, today's going to be a real sleeper. I can feel it in my bones. Why don't you take the rest of the day off—with pay?''

"I couldn't.''

"I insist. Give you some time to check out the Sunday classifieds. You'll have no problem finding a job, kiddo."

She gave him a limp smile. She knew she could find another job. That wasn't what was bothering her. What was bothering her was the return of the feeling she'd just fought out on the street. Now it was back and double in strength—the sense that the little guy had lost...and the big boys had won again.

"Truthfully, I'm relieved I don't have to move to the mall," Benny was saying. "Can't stand all the artificial lights and the noise and the plastic plants. Most of the neighboring businesses feel the same way, but some of them are going. They say 'If you can't beat 'em, join 'em.'"

Aimee walked out of the store, thinking of her brother and the chain of lawn-care franchises that'd come to Newport, cut his prices and were methodically stealing the customer base he'd worked night and day for six years to build up. She thought of Nana. She thought of herself, so small beneath Newport's rising skyline, with only her thin cardboard folder of sketches and her impossible dreams to hold on to.

And then Aimee knew the big boys were winning, because twice today already they'd made her doubt herself. She heard Benny's prophecy. *If you can't beat 'em...*

She stopped in the middle of the street. *Who says you can't beat 'em?*

She could.

Couldn't she?

Hadn't she been offered, in Vivian's own words "a once-in-a-lifetime opportunity"?

Hadn't she listened to her nana's tears, her mother's drunken laughter, and vowed her life was going to be different?

The impatient beep of a black Mercedes moved her on, but Aimee's thoughts wouldn't be so easily deterred.

Could one person without anything but a past of shame and poverty, a promise to the future and an open door to one of the country's most powerful, wealthiest families, take arms against the status quo and win?

She kept walking, not sure where she was headed. Ideas were forming, carrying her forward. She had no intentions of serious harm. She only wanted to prove a point, turn the tables, open the eyes of people like Vivian Tremont who thought human beings could be bought like day-old bread.

Why couldn't the little guy win for a change?

She walked to a pay phone on the corner before she could change her mind. She dialed and waited for the other party to be summoned to the phone. Finally there came Vivian's slightly nasal greeting. "Hello?"

With the first step taken, a sudden serenity settled over Aimee, steadied her breathing, steeled her pulse to an even beat of resolve.

"I'll do it," she said. She took a breath. "I'll marry Shawn."

There was a blood-pounding pause. Finally Vivian responded, "Of course you will, darling."

Aimee took another breath, grateful the groom was, as she'd guessed, the easier of two evils.

Then Vivian's voice, smoother than silk, came back on the line. "But first you'll seduce Colin."

Chapter Three

"Colin?" Aimee said the name, and her calm, her certainty was desecrated. "Seduce Colin?"

"That's correct," Vivian replied.

"You asked me to marry your son."

"Yes I did. Now I'm asking you to seduce my husband's child."

Aimee felt a chill as if Colin's eyes, black as the hounds of hell, were on her now, looking right through her. "I don't understand."

"I prefer not to go into details until I have your answer."

The black eyes watched and waited.

"Yes or no?" Vivian said.

Was she beaten...before she'd even begun? The black mirrors mocked her. She remembered Colin's lips curved in amusement, his body brought too close to hers as if certain she would be scared...or seduced. Anger came in the void of her vanished calm. She had no intentions of following Vivian's conditions to their end, but Colin could stand to be taught a harmless lesson or two.

"It'll be my pleasure," she said.

THE NEXT MORNING, she stood on the marble steps to the Tremont mansion. The house rose above her. The sea sounded behind her, waves rolling with a gentle sigh, mocking the panting of her heart. She carried a small purse with her driver's license, sixteen dollars, pictures of her and Jack taken at a five-and-dime photo booth, and her grandmother's gold cross. A nylon duffel bag carried clothes, some dresses of her own design plus other items necessary for her imminent introduction to society. She lifted one foot to the bottom step.

She would stay at the house under the guise of Vivian's new personal assistant. They were lucky Colin had planned to be in town off and on throughout the summer to oversee the waterfront construction, Vivian had told her. He usually spent most of his time in New York or at his cottage on Block Island.

Aimee's left foot rose and met her right.

The plan was simple, Vivian had explained. Aimee was to mislead Colin into a marriage proposal. Then, on the morning of the wedding, Aimee would really marry Shawn, leaving Colin high and dry at the altar. "What if Colin isn't interested in me?" Aimee had asked.

"That's a million-dollar question," Vivian had replied.

Aimee took another step.

Jack had sat in stunned silence when she had told him her decision last evening. She wished she could tell him more, but not yet. After she received the signed contract from Vivian, she'd take him into her confidence. For now she could only ask him to trust her.

He'd answered, "Be careful."

She'd reached the top of the stairs. She knocked, and the heavy door swung open.

There was no choice but to go forward.

COLIN WAVED AWAY the girl as she approached with the silver coffeepot. He looked at Vivian at the end of the long table. Shawn rarely rose before noon. Hugo was taking his breakfast in bed.

"I understand you've added another event to this season's social calendar?" Colin caught Vivian's gaze. "A wedding?"

Vivian eyed Colin. The rim of the Waterford goblet rested against her lips for a pulse beat, then she took a sip, savoring the sweet tang of grapefruit juice, the welcome bite of vodka. "A wedding is what Hugo wants, and I intend to oblige him."

"And the blonde you brought in Saturday night? I assume she's the blushing bride?"

Vivian smiled. "Beautiful, isn't she?"

Colin raised his china cup in mock salute. "Your taste was always impeccable, Vivian."

His stepmother took another sip, the smile never leaving her face. "It's a shame we can't say the same for your father."

Colin ignored the challenge. "Who is she?"

"The girl? She interests you?"

"Who is she? And what did you offer her to marry Shawn?"

"Don't be ridiculous, Colin. Why would I have to offer her anything? A handsome husband, instant status, plus a family fortune. These are reasons enough for any girl.''

''Then why did you choose her?''

''Colin, your desperation is inflating your imagination. I haven't chosen anyone nor do I need to. Shawn is perfectly capable of selecting a suitable mate. I don't need to play Dolly Levi. It was your father who enjoyed the theater—not me.''

Colin set down the Limoges cup on its delicate saucer. ''I intend to win this game.''

''As do I.'' Vivian took another taste of her drink, holding the liquid in her mouth for a moment, then swallowing.

Colin pushed himself away from the table. ''You may not believe it, but it's in the family's best interests that the business and all other assets are under my control.''

Vivian's laughter skittered across the table's smooth mahogany stretch. ''You're right. I don't believe it.''

Colin stood up. The carved mahogany chair tilted, but he caught it with a firm hand. ''Let the games begin.''

Vivian's smile thinned rapier sharp. ''They already have.''

''YOU'LL NEED new clothes. Put them on my account. I don't want my future daughter-in-law wearing off the rack.'' Vivian's mouth split into a smile. ''You'll have a car at your disposal, of course, and pocket money. My lawyers are drawing up the papers that will cover all the details. Expenses will be deducted later.''

She propped her elbows on the inlaid desk, resting her well-defined chin in her hands. "You'll have everything you need." Her voice was soft and flat.

Aimee's own hands lay in her lap. She tried to still their sudden tremble. Otherwise she appeared as collected as the woman opposite her. Her hands obeyed and lay quiet, their palms damp.

"There'll be no problem as long as you fulfill your terms of the agreement." Gone was the insincere smile. "Will there be a problem?"

Aimee shook her head.

"So we understand each other?" Vivian pushed her chair back from the desk.

Aimee shook her head again. "You haven't explained why it's so important Shawn marries and Colin doesn't."

Vivian leaned back in her chair. "Hugo, faced with his own mortality, is suddenly determined to guarantee the illustrious Tremont name will not die with him. This desire, typical of his godlike delusions, has prompted him to alter his will. Everything will now be left to the heir who marries first. Do you understand now?" Vivian steepled her fingers.

"If I attract Colin's interest…" Aimee thought out loud.

"Colin is desperate to maintain control of his beloved business. He needs a bride." Vivian filled in the blanks. "But on the morning of your intended nuptials, if you're off marrying my son…"

"Shawn wins, and Colin loses," Aimee concluded.

"Precisely." Vivian's features became full with triumph.

"Wouldn't it be simpler if I just marry Shawn now?" she questioned.

"Gee, wouldn't that be convenient?" Vivian mocked.

"A marriage of convenience," Aimee pointed out. "Isn't that the proposal?"

"Do you think Hugo is going to be fooled if Shawn marries before the copies of the new will have even been postmarked? He's sick, not senile."

"What if Colin has someone he's interested in?" Aimee wondered.

"The only thing Colin is interested in is the business. The only serious involvement he's had in years is with Leonard's Fortune 500 rating."

"And what does Shawn think of this arrangement?" Aimee said.

"Shawn thinks penniless playboys lack a certain appeal."

"But certainly Colin wouldn't take everything. I mean, couldn't a compromise be reached that—"

"I have spent my life compromising." Vivian spoke with a chilling calm. "It's either all or nothing. Do you understand me?"

Her eyes narrowed on Aimee.

"Perfectly." Aimee sought the same steel in her voice.

"Good."

Vivian stood and pressed a button on the wall behind her. "Colin is in town today lunching with Leonard's New England regional manager."

There was a light knock on the door, and after receiving permission, the summoned servant entered.

"Miss Rose will be staying in the green guest

room,'' Vivian told the man. She turned to Aimee.
''You'll be joining us for dinner this evening. Colin
will be there. Dinner's at eight. Dress.''

Aimee was dismissed.

She followed the servant down the wide hall and
up the circular staircase, their figures dwarfed by the
richly painted ceiling. They went down another long
hall, their footsteps muted by imported rugs. They
passed many dark doors, all of them closed. Shadows
gathered across the hall's dark panels.

''Are there any more bags?'' the servant asked as
he opened a door like all the doors they'd just passed.

Aimee shook her head as she stepped into a spa-
cious room of green-paneled walls and antique ivory
furniture. The sharp lines of a marble mantelpiece
crowned a fireplace on the far wall. Dark green damask curtains shaded the sun streaming through tall,
paned windows.

The servant opened a door leading to a large bathroom. He walked to another door, revealing an empty
closet bigger than the bedroom Aimee had left only
an hour ago on the other side of town.

''I'll have a girl sent to hang your clothes,'' the
servant offered.

''That's not necessary.''

''Are you certain, miss?''

''Yes.''

''Is there anything else I can do for you before I
go?''

''No.''

The servant walked to the door.

''Excuse me.'' Aimee stopped him. ''What's your
name?''

He turned. "I'm James, miss."

"I'm Aimee."

The servant nodded and continued toward the door.

"James?"

He turned once more. "Yes?"

She stepped hesitantly forward. "Thank you. Thank you, James."

A small smile altered the man's immobile countenance. "You're welcome, Miss Aimee."

She smiled back. "I'm just Aimee," she assured him. She turned toward the view of the ocean framed in the tall windows.

"Aimee?"

She turned toward the sound of her name. "Yes, James?"

"I hope you enjoy your stay here."

The door closed. Aimee was left alone in the large, cold room. "I plan to," she murmured, wondering if her intentions would have widened James's smile.

SHE RETURNED to the room at seven, dropping her shopping bags one by one as she headed for the chaise lounge angled by the fireplace. She'd put her purchases on her own account at the boutique. She didn't want to owe Vivian anything. Besides, she only needed a few accessories. The dresses she'd designed and other outfits she'd brought would get her through the upcoming events.

She sank into cool silk, resting her hand against the chair's smooth surface. She closed her eyes, soothed by the sound of running water.

Her eyes opened. Her head swiveled toward the

bathroom door. Someone was taking a shower in the bathroom. Her bathroom.

She sprang off the couch, her gaze still glued to the bathroom door. The water stopped. She didn't know who was in her bathroom or why, but whoever it was wouldn't be dressed for guests.

She gathered her trail of bags and started toward the door. Too late she heard the doorknob to the bathroom door turning. There was another door, half-open, to her left. The bathroom door began to swing open. Quickly she stepped to the left, slipping out of sight as footsteps sounded on the room's cool tile.

She stood behind the door, clutching her bags. Her breaths were soundless, but her heart beat loud. As her eyes adjusted to the darkness, she saw the pale forms of men's tailored shirts, the dark lengths of pants, the glint of a belt buckle, all confirming she was in the wrong room. Footsteps came toward the closet. The door opened farther. She moved back, pressing against the far wall. Her breathing stopped. Her eyes squeezed tight.

She heard the rustle of clothes, then the footsteps moved away.

She opened one eye, then the other. The door was still ajar. A narrow crack revealed the length of a man. A towel was draped around his middle, then dropped as he walked to the dresser. His hair glistened like the night's rain. Drops of water anointed his solid shoulders. The man bent and straightened. Aimee watched a single droplet trail down his rigid spine, scoring the unmarred square of muscle.

Colin. His name released in her breath.

He pulled on his trousers, shrouding the length of

his thighs, the corded clamp of his calves. He buttoned a shirt, white against the darkness of his skin and the shine of his damp hair. She watched the play of muscles beneath the cotton, the dance of power and strength across his back as he buttoned the shirt. He lifted an arm to button a cuff, the side of his shoulder swelling. The arm dropped. The muscle stayed taut. He walked from the room without so much as a glance in the mirror, the fit of his clothes only teasing at the untainted masculinity Aimee now knew.

The bedroom door closed, and she dropped her head. Expecting relief, the sigh she took caught and trembled. All the cold calm she had courted was gone. The calculating certainty, the controlled determination were destroyed, shattered by the man just seen. She felt only a loneness, followed by a complete reversal of the decisions she had reasoned. Emotion washed over her like the waves beyond the bedroom window. She was afraid.

She closed her eyes, overwhelmed. Behind her closed lids, she saw Colin's figure, naked, proud, unrepentant in its manliness. A feeling purer than fear, stronger than doubt shook her. And she was rocked, mired, melting in desire.

Her head fell back against the wall. The bags dropped to her feet. She opened her eyes, blinking in the darkness, banishing the longing, the bold yearning. She had to get out of here, out of this closet awash with the subtle scent of man, out of this room where Colin walked, slept, dreamed dark dreams. She picked up her bags and opened the closet door. Desire dissolved; determination returned.

It was a physical reaction, she assured herself as she made her way down the hall. Perfectly normal, she decided as she tried to find the door to her bedroom. Her third try was successful. She looked around, making sure she wasn't wrong. Once certain she was right, she set down her purse and slowed her breathing. There, in the stillness, her thoughts wouldn't be denied.

She'd come here to teach a lesson to those who wielded their power unfairly, to prove human beings are to be loved, not bought and sold. But wasn't she herself tempted? Didn't she, maybe for a moment, imagine the things that could be bought, the life that could be led with a million dollars? Just now, didn't desire take her like a pleading voice? Lust and greed lived in this house, but they lived in her heart, as well.

She'd come here to teach others a lesson, but she also would learn.

Colin had caught her off guard. From now on, she'd have to be careful to keep her guard up at all times. She'd already come too far. Vivian wanted to win. Colin wanted to win. Shawn wanted to win.

But she alone had to win.

THE OTHERS WERE SEATED by the time she reached the dining room. The men stood. At the head of the long mahogany table was Hugo. To his right, midway down the table, was Colin, his clothing a black-and-white contrast beneath the brass chandelier's subdued glow. Opposite Colin was Shawn in off-white cashmere and pleated trousers of neutral beige.

"Aimee, please join us," Vivian invited from the

other far end of the table. Her hair was rolled in a perfect ash-blond coil, so tight it pulled at her features, giving her face a strained look. Beneath navy linen, her full breasts were secured high. "Place Aimee next to me," she instructed the butler.

All eyes watched Aimee walk to the chair pulled out for her by the tall, thin man in tails. "Looking good, James," she whispered.

James replied with a quick wink, the action pulling his mouth up into a half smile.

She sat down and faced the Tremont family. She was wearing one of her designs—a simple, sleeveless A-line sheath of bright yellow silk. She had colored her mouth pale pink and hoped she looked the picture of propriety.

She took in the snow-white stretch of heavy damask, the elaborate silver settings of forks, spoons and knives in various sizes. Plates and bowls of gold-edged china nested between the flatware. A cut-crystal goblet was filled with water. A thinner version waited for wine. Gold candelabra cast whispers of light across the room's rubbed-ruby paneling. A low Wedgwood bowl of white roses was centered on the table, their scent welcomingly overpowering.

"Wow," Aimee said.

There were low, not unkind chuckles. "We do tend to put on the dog at dinnertime, don't we, dear girl?" Hugo said to his guest. "You'll have to excuse our affected ways. We tend to think of ourselves as more important than we really are. It's the curse of the very rich."

"Oh, no, I didn't mean…" Aimee twisted the triangle of tablecloth above her lap. "Everything's so lovely and...do you eat like this every night?'' she blurted.

Vivian's laughter flowed from the end of the table. ''I'm afraid so.''

A servant began to fill the gilt-edged bowls with a clear broth.

''I take it your family is a little less ostentatious?'' Hugo asked.

''One Thanksgiving, I remember, there was a turkey of tissue paper. You unfolded one end and his tail spread like a big fan.... You know what I mean?'' She twisted the corner of the tablecloth.

Vivian smiled her ever-gracious hostess smile. ''I don't think we've ever had a paper turkey.''

''Oh, no, I didn't mean...I mean, you'd probably just have a big ol' bird bronzed or something.''

The rich rumble of Colin's laughter filled the room, mingling with the glows of candlelight, crystal, silver and gold.

Aimee ventured a glance and saw, for the first time, a light in the smoldering depths of those dark eyes. The stiff set of his shoulders had relaxed to a comfortable curve.

''We usually have an arrangement of asters and tiger lilies for our Thanksgiving centerpiece,'' Vivian said.

The low peal of Colin's laughter lingered in the room. Hugo was also smiling warmly; Shawn's grin was too broad. Aimee reached for her linen napkin and smoothed it several times across her lap. She ignored her soup, not trusting her hands to hold a spoon steady.

She reached for the goblet of water, meeting

Colin's curious, black stare. She took several sips. As the others began their meal, Vivian leaned over and whispered, "Relax. We're not going to eat you alive."

Aimee smiled. Like hell, she thought. The lawyers were drawing up the papers even now as the Tremonts sat smiling, their features soft in the muted light and their shadows dancing across the polished walls.

A servant removed the soup bowls, replacing them with a gilded plate. In its center, in a small sea of butter, sat a black mushroom, thinly sliced. Aimee was still staring at it when Colin spoke.

"It seems," he addressed Aimee, "Vivian intends to make you earn your keep around here."

She was forced to meet the flat black challenge of his eyes.

"Aimee has accepted the position of my personal assistant," Vivian interceded.

"So your function will be to assist Vivian with her personal aims?"

Aimee's gaze held steady for only a moment, then dropped. She was no match for this man.

"I expect Aimee will prove indispensable to me before the summer is over," Vivian answered.

Aimee was grateful for the intrusion of the server. She studied the scoop of pink ice set before her. It's a good thing she wasn't hungry. They'd only had soup and some fungus.

"Excuse me," she said to the young girl serving. "I don't care for any dessert, thank you."

The table was quiet. "It's sorbet," Vivian informed. "To cleanse your palate."

"Oh," Aimee muttered. Her lashes lowered. Her face flushed.

Colin broke the silence. "I don't care for any, either." He pushed away the small silver bowl.

"Yes, I suppose my palate's clean enough, thank you." Hugo handed back the ice to the servant. The girl looked around the table in confusion.

"Sir?" she asked Shawn, offering the tray.

He shrugged. "I guess not."

"Just clear," Vivian, obviously annoyed, ordered the girl. "And bring out the main course."

Aimee reached for her water glass, meeting again Colin's gaze. A curious gleam reflected in the darkness of his eyes. If score was being kept, she'd have no idea who was winning. But it definitely wasn't her.

"Vivian will also be helping me launch my career in women's fashion," she announced.

To her credit, Vivian didn't even risk an extra blink. Hugo and Shawn looked up with interest. Colin's curious study stayed on Aimee.

"I know we promised to keep it a secret until I finish all the sketches," she said to Vivian. "But I'm just so excited," she told the rest of the table.

"I'm sure Vivian can be very influential in connecting you with the right people in and outside of the industry," Hugo noted.

"She's even offered to wear some of my designs," Aimee told him. She thought she heard a muted gurgle from the other end of the table.

"She's been so generous." Aimee still spoke to Hugo, but her words were meant for the others. "She's giving me the opportunity of a lifetime."

Vivian sounded a light, high laugh. "Your success will be my reward, dear girl."

"But I intend to also enjoy the rewards of my hard work," Aimee replied. "I know it won't be easy, but I'm sure it'll be worth it."

She stopped the servant reaching for the sorbet. "Perhaps I'll try this after all. Since Vivian is going to make me a rich woman, I might as well start acting like one." She lifted a spoonful of the pink ice, tasting it with a flick of her tongue. She licked her lips. "Yes, I could get used to this."

Across the table, Colin's eyes hardened to onyx.

AFTER DINNER, she'd avoided Vivian by accepting Hugo's invitation to teach her backgammon. She'd lost the first two games, and although she'd won the third, she knew Hugo had let her win. She'd then gone for a walk down by the sea, the full moon reflecting off the water, turning the darkness to gray gauze.

Her thoughts turned, of their own will, to Colin. Shawn amused her; Hugo encouraged her; Vivian tolerated her. But Colin confused her with feelings so new, she had no name for them. The very thought of him assaulted her, subdued her, left her shaking, sent her soaring. One glance from those midnight eyes, and she questioned everything she'd planned, and right and wrong became as gray as the night surrounding her.

She lifted her face to the full moon. Was she doing the right thing? The moon stared blankly back at her, its secrets safe behind its pale sheen.

It was after midnight when she returned and walked up the back terrace's stone steps.

She saw the small red round glow first, then heard the words, "That's quite an offer Vivian made you." She recognized Colin's voice before her eyes adjusted to the darkness. Gradually his sharp, dark outline was revealed. He was seated in one of the white wrought-iron chairs past the row of French doors. The glowing red circle burned brighter for a moment, then dulled. Aimee smelled the mask of cigar smoke mingling with the sea's own rich promise.

The circle burned bright once more as he waited for her reply.

Colin couldn't know about the million dollars, could he? She felt the erratic pull of fear. How would he have found out?

"Excuse me?" Her voice was a stranger's, convincingly confused.

He stood and came toward her, his figure darker than the night. "You must be very pleased Vivian has taken such a personal interest in you."

"Yes." Please let him be talking about Vivian's offer to help with her design career, Aimee hoped. "Once-in-a-lifetime opportunity." Her throat constricted with the forced flippancy in her voice.

"Once-in-a-lifetime, indeed." Colin's dark features were severed by a smile. "I'm sure by the end of the summer, you'll be a raging success."

"I understand you're staying on for the summer also?" She attempted to alter the conversation's course.

"I'll be back and forth between here and New

York over the next few months to supervise the construction of the mall.''

In the night, there was only the white of his eyes, the glow of the cigar, the width of his darkly drawn form. It was impossible to know what was real and what was innuendo. What will he do when she reveals her real purpose here? she wondered. Would the sparks she glimpsed occasionally in his black irises lengthen to lights of admiration? Or steel daggers of scorn?

"Would you like to sit down?" he invited.

"I'm very tired," she said, speaking the truth. Tomorrow, when she could easily watch his eyes, his expression, she would begin her false pursuit of him. Here, under the cloak of darkness, he had all the advantages.

"I imagine Vivian will insist you attend the Preservation Society's dinner tomorrow night."

"She hasn't mentioned it."

"I'm sure she will. It's the perfect platform for her to start introducing her protégée to the cream of Newport society. Let's cut her off at the pass and go together."

His invitation was unexpected and, for a moment, Aimee said nothing.

"Think of it. If you can persuade Colin Tremont to make an appearance on your arm, the society queens will be convinced of your powers to charm the savage beast. They'll gather round you, demanding your secrets of allurement." He smiled in the darkness. "Of course, we'll tell them it's the drape of the chiffon, the come-hither sheen of silk, the simple crease of cotton."

Aimee eyed him. He was taunting her, but to what purpose? "I'll go."

His smile became fuller in the darkness. "I promise we'll only have to make an appearance, then, perhaps, we can have a quiet dinner together."

It was definitely to be a date, she realized. He suggested a time, and she again agreed, then said a lyrical good-night. She went inside and made her way along the halls dressed in shadows. She undressed without turning on the light, fearing her false face in the mirror. She crawled between sheets of Irish weave. That was too easy, she thought.

On the terrace, Colin stood in the night's cloak. The air was sweet and heavy with the garden's well-tended bounty. The breeze was slight, soft, and the sea's call quiet. Content men were sleeping.

He inhaled deeply, turning the cigar's ash orange. Above the cigar's hot glow, his eyes narrowed. That was too easy, he thought.

In the sky above, the moon kept its silent counsel.

Chapter Four

Aimee was summoned to Vivian's office the next morning. The door was open when she arrived at the high-ceiling room. Beyond the room's tall windows was the garden. There was a man kneeling beside a white rose bush, removing its spent blooms. Aimee assumed it was the gardener. She thought of her brother. The man straightened, took off his baseball cap and wiped his brow, his hair midnight in the sun. It was Colin.

Vivian looked up from an opened appointment book. The muscles in her face tightened. Little lines appeared along her upper lip.

"Gather your things and get out." She adjusted her half glasses and returned her attention to the leather-bound book.

Only a step inside the door, Aimee stopped. The words *"I don't understand"* immediately rose within her but went no farther. She did understand. She'd overstepped her boundaries too early. She'd been careless. Now it'd cost her. She stood in the threshold.

Vivian didn't look up. "Goodbye."

Not yet, Aimee thought. *Not before its even begun.*

"Goodbye?" she questioned. "You aren't going to the Preservation Society's dinner dance this evening?"

Vivian looked up. "Of course I'm going. I'm on the board."

"Then this isn't 'Goodbye.' It's 'Until then.'"

Vivian removed her half glasses. Closing her eyes, she rubbed the bridge of her nose. Glassy sunlight from the side windows angled across her features. "What are you talking about?" Her eyes stayed closed.

Aimee stepped closer to the desk. "Colin asked me to go with him."

Vivian's eyes opened, flat and assessing. "Damn you," she said.

Aimee slid into a chair's soft leather. She lowered her voice to a conspirator's tone. "You're not pleased?"

Vivian's hands splayed across the desk, her fingertips leaving little clouds where they touched the glass top. Her eyes were on Aimee. She spoke in the undertone of threat.

"I'm willing to attribute last night's display at dinner to the eager enthusiasm of an amateur. Obviously your assertion I'll be launching you as the next Coco Chanel was a ploy to fend off Colin's apparent suspicions."

She didn't wait for Aimee to answer. "What other motive would you have for forfeiting one million dollars?"

Now she waited for an answer. Aimee said nothing, hoping her silence would be understood as agreement.

"Have I made a mistake?" Vivian wondered for Aimee's benefit. "It seems Colin doesn't think so." Her hand lifted, seeking the reassuring curve of her perfectly coiffed head.

"I'll forgive you." Her hand, threaded with blue veins and soft from creams and care, made a generous sweep of dismissal.

Aimee stood and started toward the door.

"But..." Vivian's voice stopped her. Aimee turned back to the women captured in the sun's cruel glare.

"I won't forget."

Past Vivian, outside the windows, Aimee saw Colin was gone, might never have been except for the scattering of white rose petals along the grass's green nap.

SHE WORE her version of the basic black dress to the evening benefit. The slim dress began with a ring of black crepe around the neck, then went sheer across the shoulders and sleeves. In it, Aimee, her legs nylon sheathed, the arch of her foot boldly angled by tall heels, almost believed she belonged as she moved among the elite that evening. Guests spilled out like sprinkled jewels on to the veranda and sloping grounds of the Bellevue Avenue estate. Aimee was at the party over forty-five minutes before she saw Vivian.

Vivian saw her at the same time, her reaction immediate. Her eyebrows lifted, then lowered, her mouth turned up in approval. For a moment, Aimee thought it was her classic dress that pleased her intended mother-in-law. Then she realized Colin had returned to her side. He'd been detained by a man smelling of bourbon and Burberry. Aimee had been pulled away by the push of the crowd. Colin took her arm now, anchoring her against the crush of guests. Aimee saw Vivian's smile grow wider.

"Aimee! Colin!" she exclaimed when she reached them. Her lips air-kissed their cheeks. "I'm so glad you two decided to come together. The dinner is for such a good cause, although how the Randalls—" she smiled at their hosts several feet away "—ever managed to get on the Preservation Society's board is beyond me."

Colin looked around the lavish room. "I'm sure they took advantage of an old Newport tradition and bought their way in." His gaze came back to Vivian. "Isn't that the way it's done? If you want something, and you can pay the price, it's yours?"

He was grasping, and he could see by the amused expression on Vivian's face she knew it. But he was confused by Aimee's easy agreement to a date, by Vivian's apparent approval of their pairing. The crowd seemed to be swelling around them. The lighting was too dim.

"Colin, don't be crude." Vivian dismissed his challenge.

The trio was joined by a woman with silver tints in her hair. "Is Colin being crude again?" The twinkle of silver was in her pale gray eyes also. "Good for him."

"Millie, you know Colin." Vivian's features remained fixed in a smile. "He refuses to be refined.

He was just speculating how the Randalls bought their seats on the society board.''

The old woman laughed. Aimee could see the glint of gold in her back teeth. ''Of course they did. Too bad they didn't save some of their money to buy some taste. There's enough silk fringe in this room alone to hang half of Newport.''

Vivian agreed with a sigh. ''Their decorating is rather...controversial.''

The other woman selected a piece of dry toast with peanut butter and bacon bits from an offered tray. ''At least they got the appetizers right. But if they serve anything but a clear broth for the first course, they might as well start packing their bags. You do remember the McAllister fiasco last year, don't you?'' she asked Vivian. ''They served that thick, sweet soup.'' Millie shuddered as she nibbled at a corner of toast. ''Their house was on the market two weeks later.''

''Excuse us.'' Without waiting for permission, Colin led Aimee away. He steered her toward the door.

''We're leaving?''

''Yes. If I stay one second longer, I'll be the first to swing from that silk fringe.''

Aimee stopped. ''That's it? One drink, and a sneer or two, which you obviously think passes as smooth small talk?''

He reached for her hand. ''You're forgetting I also promised you dinner.''

She shook his hand off. ''You're a lousy date. Has anyone ever told you that?''

He faced the fire in her eyes. ''Yes.'' He smiled.

"There are a few women in this room alone who'd love to see me test out those silk tassels."

"Start the list with me."

His smile only widened.

"Although I'll probably have to fight Vivian for that honor."

His smile broke open with laughter. "Is there anyone else here I should add?"

His amusement sapped her anger. "That depends. Do you think we can get to the car without you offending anyone?"

His lips remained in an easy curve. "So, you are ready to go?"

"You could've asked me that five minutes ago."

His smile softened, saying he was sorry. "You're right. That was rude. Are you ready to leave?"

"Yes, I am." She swept by him, a smooth movement of dark and light.

He caught up with her by the time they reached the porch.

"Why'd you come here tonight if you hate this sort of thing so much?" she asked as they went down the steps.

He looked at her, the pearl radiance of the full moon on her features. *Why did* you *come here?* He wanted to return the question. *When you were chosen for Shawn?* Confusion came on him once more. He banished it with a turn of his head away from the woman with the false face of an angel. He handed his ticket to the waiting valet.

"But isn't this what you want?" he answered, arms opening wide, gesturing at the seemingly unbroken row of mansions surrounding them. He saw her facial muscles tense and the flame in her eye leap. "Isn't this what everyone wants?" He moved from the specific to the general. "To penetrate society's inner sanctum?"

Aimee looked to the high walls bordering the estates. She gazed into the darkness outside the iron grilles.

"Stand outside those walls and look in," she said. "You'll see the homes too big to be lived in, the woman so carefully tended, the men moving in a world fueled by their own wealth and power. Is it so surprising those standing out there are drawn like a starving man hungers? To desire isn't a crime."

Colin thought of his father. He looked at the woman. Did she desire? Had she been seduced with the promise of enviable riches?

"Even if desire leads to destruction?" he demanded of her. "I stand inside these walls, and I don't see castles, but white elephants, relics of a time long gone when Newport was considered America's social capital. I see old-timers suspended in their glory days, hanging on to their past with well-bred vengeance. They're charming at the dinner parties. They'll eat the food, drink the wine, but when they go home, they laugh at the newcomers with their new money and their paid-for airs. What they don't realize is they're equally ridiculous. Developers are ripping down their world all around them, but the old guard just continues—Newport in the summer, Palm Beach in the winter, croquet with everyone dressed in summer whites, a cabana on Bailey's Beach. Society's inner sanctum." A tight laugh spilled. "Society's inner insanity is more like it."

Aimee heard the cries beneath Colin's words, cries she recognized from a childhood in which there were more cruel words than kind, in which he didn't belong, but he didn't belong anywhere else, either. She looked at this man darkened by the night and need. She saw him kneeling beside the white roses, tending their delicate demands.

She shouldn't touch him. She wouldn't be able to think with his flesh beneath her fingers. She would only feel a sensation softer than the summer air surrounding them, older than the ocean waves lapping at the land. Still her hand reached out.

He caught it. His voice was yielding. "At the risk of losing my reputation as a lousy date, we can go back inside if you'd like."

She saw sincerity in the dark eyes that usually gave away nothing. She turned from him, saying nothing, not knowing what she wanted anymore.

"Or how about dinner at a quiet restaurant? A walk along the beach? A midnight flight to Cancún?"

She felt the start of a smile. "Stop teasing me."

"I'm not teasing you," he insisted. He brought her hand up, pulling her in closer to him. She saw the shadow of freshly shaven skin. She smelled his scent like new life. "I only want to please you."

"Why?" She had to ask.

"When it comes to the heart, there's very little rhyme or reason." He pulled her to him. She felt his power, his strength. "Or do you take a more practical approach to love?"

She tilted her head back, matching his watchful gaze. "Which would you prefer?"

"Can you be so easily persuaded to either position?" The dark eyes were again smooth.

Her chin lifted higher, bringing her lips closer to his. "Which would make you turn away?"

He spoke, his breath caressing her skin. "Which would make you stay?"

His nearness took over her senses. Her words were a whisper. "I'm here now."

"You'll stay?" He spoke with hushed need.

"I'm here now." Her lips parted, begging to be kissed.

He hesitated, a mad craving coming into his eyes before they turned opaque. His hands dropped to her waist, then fell away from her. He stepped back, breaking the embrace. Aimee felt the night air against her skin. A cold finger drew down her spine. The car arrived.

"So…?" Colin took the car keys and tipped the boy. He stood in shadow from her. The dark angles of his face blended with the night. "Did you decide what you want to do?"

"This," Aimee declared. She stepped back into the warm circle of his body's heat, her mouth taking his in passionate promise. She closed her eyes, seeing the same darkness that drew her to this man and knowing it was as blinding as love's bright light. Still, she didn't stop.

She kissed him, this man so sure she would be scared or seduced. She was both, her play for power ending as soon as his lips touched hers. His mouth was open, expecting her. His tongue came inside, filled her mouth's hollow, and all the rules were broken. Motives left, leaving only need.

Her body pressed against him, alive and un-ashamed with desire. Her mouth opened wider, hun-gry. She could taste his strength and power, the cruel circle of his mouth, the hot demand of his body.

Her hands held fast to the width of his back. There was no give in his flesh, no slack in his muscles. Her fingers ran down the hard line of his arms, meeting his own hands. Their palms pressed against each other, the force causing their arms to rise up like wings.

His tongue went deeper, reaching for the unreach-able recesses inside her. His mouth moved on hers in insatiable seduction. *Whisper me your secrets,* it seemed to say.

She pulled away in one last grasp for control. She drew back her head, her eyes meeting his. Their palms stayed pressed together in equal, flat force.

His lips were slightly opened, seeking breath. The desire in his eyes was dusted with challenge. His power was a tangible thing, triumphant in the silence. In his arms she had felt his strength, mistaken it for her own. When she pulled away, it was gone, given back to him, leaving her drained, breathless. He watched her, seeing her chest rise and fall too quickly. She didn't know if she'd just made an ally or an enemy. She let her hands drop first.

"You'll stay," he said. It was no longer a ques-tion.

"No, no. You hit the ball through the hoop—not around it." Shawn's tone was exasperated, but his smile was full.

Aimee received his comment with a pixie's grin. "Did I at least hit the right color ball?" she asked.

Shawn shook his mallet at her, his beautifully boyish smile splitting wide open. A less wiser woman would have been disarmed. "We take our croquet very seriously around here," he advised her.

She let her amusement out in rippling laughter. "So I've heard."

Shawn propped his hands on his hips. The mallet stuck out from his side at a forty-five-degree angle. "How am I ever going to get you ready for the Casino if you aren't going to cooperate? I don't suppose you play tennis?"

"About as well as I play croquet."

The mallet rose heavenward as Shawn lifted his arms in defeat. "It's a lost cause," he told a seagull flying above.

Aimee laughed again. "I'm sorry I'm such a great disappointment to you."

He looked at her with the smile he had perfected. "No, never. You're more than I ever dreamed of."

"Right." The laughter was still in her voice. "Me and about two-thirds of the women within ten miles of here."

His eyebrows rose in a pretense of shock. "You doubt my sincerity?"

"No," Aimee assured him. "I think you actually believe what you're saying…each time you say it…to each different girl you say it to."

"Finally, a woman who understands me." Shawn dropped to his knees. "Marry me," he proposed with exaggerated passion.

The smile on Aimee's face suddenly ached. She

felt the corners of her mouth come down. "You'd better get up. You'll get grass stains on your white pants."

Shawn stood up and draped an arm loosely around her shoulders. In his other hand, he swung the mallet back and forth. "You'll make some man a wonderful wife," he said, steering her toward the next arced hoop.

She stiffened.

"I understand it's to be me."

She moved out of the curve of his arm. "I think I've had enough of a lesson today."

"Too late. Here comes my grandfather, and he's got the backgammon board."

Aimee turned, but before she saw Hugo, her eye caught a figure on the second-floor balcony. Silhouetted in shadow, she saw Colin's lean outline. The sun grew too hot, seeping into her. Beads of sweat formed along her upper lip. This was the first time she'd seen him since last night.

After they'd left the party, they'd eaten at the nearly empty dining room of The Clam Company. Colin had sent his swordfish back twice before resigning himself to a mediocre meal. Aimee's shrimp wasn't much better, but the ocean outside their window compensated for the food.

The endless splendor of the sea, however, couldn't make up for the awkward conversation between the couple. There were too many silences spliced together with banal comments and halting replies. Emotion seemed to have thickened their tongues and overpowered their speech.

There should never have been that kiss between

them, Aimee realized. Nor any touches, embraces or even gazes that met and dissolved the distance separating them. Maybe if they'd met another way, in another world. But she'd been bought to steal away his inheritance. She was only too aware of her promise to Vivian, a promise she never planned to carry out, but still it was there, hanging like a noose above her head.

Colin was aware of something, too. She saw the skepticism in his eyes, the mockery in his smile. Yet he'd asked her out, and she'd said yes. Then they'd wrapped their arms about each other and held fast.

She'd never meant more than to eliminate the taunt that turned his mouth hard. Contrary to her promise to Vivian, she never intended to do him harm. She had always planned to tell him the whole truth as soon as she signed the contract. Any revelations before that were too big a risk, and Vivian had made it clear she wouldn't tolerate one more mistake.

So Aimee had sat across the linen-decked table and looked into black eyes reflecting her own image and vowed not to make one more mistake.

Colin stood like a sentry above her now. She knew what he saw—her in sky-blue gauze and a wide-brimmed hat, Shawn swaggering in white, chasing little balls across the green stretch of grass. She couldn't see Colin's face, but she knew his lips would be tight with contempt, his jaw angled with disdain. He didn't wave. She looked away, chills competing against a feverish flush.

Hugo was being pushed toward her. Tiring easily, he used a wheelchair whenever he went outside.

Across his lap was the wooden backgammon box. Aimee glanced back up at the roof. Colin was gone.

"You people sure do like to play a lot of games," she said to Shawn standing beside her.

COLIN LEFT for New York Sunday evening, needing to take care of several company matters before he returned later in the week to meet with the engineers and architects involved in the mall project. Aimee began her duties as Vivian's assistant, running errands, addressing envelopes, making appointments, answering the phone.

On Wednesday, when Aimee carried the morning mail into Vivian's office, she found her with a man seated on the settee. A briefcase was opened on the carved tea table, and Vivian and the man were reviewing a thick document.

"Here she is now," Vivian said as Aimee set the opened mail on her desk. "Aimee, this is my lawyer."

The heavyset man stood up and offered his hand. "Miss Rose."

"Sit down, Aimee," Vivian instructed. "The contracts are ready to be signed."

Aimee sat down on Queen Anne curves and took the copy of the contract offered to her by the lawyer.

"Miss Rose, I understand you and Mrs. Tremont have discussed and already agreed to the terms set forth in this document, but look it over a moment. I'll be happy to answer any questions."

She leafed through the pages. The language was complex legalese, but she was able to make out the million dollars Vivian had promised would be hers, provided she met the terms set forth in the contract.

She looked up at Vivian and the lawyer watching her. "I'll sign."

She took the pen the lawyer offered and wrote her name beneath Vivian's elegant script. She looked up, meeting the triumph in Vivian's eyes, a triumph that would be challenged.

The lawyer promised to fax copies of the contract that afternoon, and left. Vivian walked him to the door, then returned.

"Well." She pressed her hands together, the flush of success still in her cheeks. "I'll admit you had me worried in the beginning, but your actions the past few days have made it clear you're willing to co-operate."

Aimee just smiled.

"Colin called Hugo last night. He's coming in from New York late today. I want you to join us for dinner again this evening. In fact, take the rest of the day and do some shopping—get your hair done, get a facial, a manicure, buy something stunning. My treat." Vivian's lips almost approached a smile.

"Thank you." Aimee was equally gracious.

"There's one other thing," Vivian said, sitting down at her desk. "I'll need some sketches of dresses or whatever."

The request surprised Aimee. "Why?"

"It seems Hugo was intrigued by your ludicrous suggestion I'm involving myself in your career aspirations. I have the suspicion Colin is encouraging him. Anyway, I need something on paper for credibility's sake. If you sew something up, all the better.

If necessary, I'll even wear one of your things to dinner one night, but hopefully things won't get that out of hand.''

The contract signed, Aimee could even smile at the woman's boundless audacity. ''You've not even seen my talents, Vivian. You might be surprised.''

The woman sat back against tufted cushions, her blue-veined hands folded on the desk. ''I make it a strict policy never to be surprised.''

Aimee left, still smiling. The contract had been signed, giving her a weapon against a world that didn't like to lose...and rarely did.

She could also tell Colin the truth now. She'd risk his reaction. She'd suffer his scorn, bear his anger. It was a small price to pay not to have to lie to him any longer. She'd thought he needed to be taught a lesson, but the lesson had been hers to learn. She could no longer feel indignation when he smiled with wickedness, and his body boldly came too near, certain she would be scared or seduced. She could. One kiss, and his victory had been complete.

No, the contract had been signed, freeing one Tremont, imprisoning another. She'd officially open fire tonight at dinner. She reached her bedroom and found her purse propped against a vanity table leg. As she picked it up, she saw her sketch pad on the secretary in the corner. She had a million things to do before tonight. Still, her sketch pad beckoned as if aware of Vivian's request. Maybe she'd sit a moment, doodle one dress. She set down the purse, found a pencil and opened her pad to an earlier work-in-progress. She began to draw and erase, then draw some more, her random zigzags taking shape into bold, sure lines. A few minutes later, she had a long, angular silhouette draped in a mid-calf tunic.

She leaned back, critiquing her work. She flipped over to a blank sheet. She put her pencil to the paper. For the first time in many days, she was content.

Chapter Five

Colin wasn't scheduled to return to Newport until Thursday.

He came back on Wednesday.

In between, three days had been wasted, reports unfinished, meetings ended without resolution. Three days with only thoughts of Newport. And it wasn't the broad lawns reaching to the bay or the curve of the sand against the sea that drew him. Nor was he thinking of the early morning, so still, the lobstermen could be heard pulling their traps offshore. He didn't think of the lull between afternoon and evening when responsibilities waned, or the nights no more than the rhythm of the waves.

He thought of Aimee.

Why not? he reasoned. "Why not?" he said out loud as he crossed the Rhode Island state line. Wasn't the acquisition of a wife his number one business priority? Forget net profit margins or projected overseas expansion. The fate of the Tremont retail empire and its employees rested in the hands of one woman, one man…and the negotiation of a contract. A contract of marriage.

The background report Human Resources had prepared on his potential bride had neither eased nor confirmed his thoughts. Their information listed several jobs, all in the retail area except for some part-time work in a landscaping business operated by her brother. She'd also taken several night courses in design and retail at the community college. About a year ago she'd started working at a small boutique on Thames Street. There'd been nothing incriminating about the report. No bad employer references, no bad credit reports, no outstanding traffic tickets, not even a fine for an overdue library book.

Had he been wrong about her? Colin wondered. Had his ingrained suspicions gotten the best of him? Was it possible Aimee was no more than what she said: Vivian's newly hired personal assistant, a former shop clerk, a fledgling dress designer?

If so, he owed her a very big apology.

Still, he couldn't dismiss the wariness rivaling his thoughts of apology and understanding. He couldn't help it. He'd been born a Tremont.

THE SUN HAD STARTED its descent when Aimee sprinted down the terrace steps. She ran as if being chased, but there was no one behind her. She was driven only by the news she'd heard minutes ago: Colin had come home.

She had searched the house until James had suggested she try the workshop in the back of the carriage house. She hurried past the forever-watching carved figures around the fountain. Beyond a stand of trees she saw the carriage house. It grew bigger with each determined step she took.

How angry would Colin be at her deception? Her steady steps hesitated as the building came closer. She could almost see the fury gathering in his eyes, the rage raking his expression. She stared at the twin arches in front of her. The entrance doors were tall and looked heavy. She didn't know what lay beyond them. She only knew she had to go through them.

She leaned her shoulder against one door and pushed. It swung slowly as she stepped through it. It closed behind her with a groan. She didn't move for several seconds, disorientated by the darkness.

Gradually her eyes adjusted to the gloomy interior. The building was originally used to house horse-drawn carriages. Now it'd become an enormous catchall, a junk closet of the very rich. Tools hung along the beams. Unused bicycles leaned against the walls. Boxes and steamer trunks were piled high. An old-fashioned sled, charming beneath its coating of dust, occupied one far corner. Flies zigzagged in the filmy light.

Aimee squinted into the gloom, spying a figure at the other end of the warehouse. Far back, where a row of clean windows framed unspoiled sunshine, she saw Colin.

She started slowly toward him. She couldn't see his features—only a silhouette outlined against the bright light. But she recognized the powerful arc of his back bent toward his work. She watched the sure, strong motion of his arms as he sanded a length of wood. She didn't need to see his face. She already knew the unrelenting strength of his movements, the compelling confidence of his masculinity.

She came closer, Colin's features coming into

clear relief. His profile was a painting of dark hues
and shadowy planes against the sunlight. Her sneak-
ers made no sound as she walked along the saw-
dusted concrete.

She watched him pick up a small knife and carefully carve the end of the long stalk of wood. His
eyes focused only on the lumber. Concentration softened the pupils to black velvet. The strained line of
his mouth, the taut check of his jaw were gone. He
licked his lips once, then settled them into a calm
curve. His shoulders eased into a comfortable slump.
He cut the wood, his arm muscles moving in an easy
ripple. He held the piece lightly but firmly, bowing
close after each cut to blow away the chip. Then he
touched the cut edge with a single healing stroke.

Aimee studied this man working in the silent sunlight. She didn't see the man she'd first met—the
man whose smile was a twist of scorn, whose words
ricocheted with disdain. Before her she saw only a
man whose small smile had no malice, no double
entendre. She saw a man with an aura of contentment
ringing him like the bold beam of sunlight bathing
his body.

"Colin," she called softly to the new man. He
looked up. Their eyes locked. His smile of genuine
happiness lingered for a moment. Then it was gone.
His face became smooth and hard like the wood he
held so reverently between his palms.

"Hello," he answered. His smile returned with
false finesse.

She stepped forward. "I've been looking for you."

He laid down the piece of wood. "Here I am."
The smile was too easy. Aimee searched the face

before her, looking for the man she'd seen only seconds ago. Where had he gone? He was the man she wanted to talk to.

"So you wanted me?" Colin prompted. The voice was buttery; the words inviting. The man she had glimpsed moments ago had disappeared. But she couldn't forget him. She could still see him. Where had he gone? Would he be back?

"I've got something to tell you." She spoke to the face she knew was a fake.

"Sounds serious," he teased.

"It could've been," she allowed.

A frown pulled his brows together. "Please, sit down." He moved over on the bench.

She ignored his offer. She looked away, meeting the brilliance of the sun. When she looked back, sun spots danced across Colin's concerned face. She couldn't tell if his caring expression was real or pretense. She'd seen too many faces on this man.

"Hugo wants an heir, a great-grandchild."

He looked away from her and reached for his wood. His face was impassive. "Sorry, darling, but around here that's not exactly a state secret."

"Vivian hired me to do it."

His surprise was so complete she could feel it. He set down the wood and faced her, stony judgment in his features. She took a deep breath, preparing to tell him the whole story—the proposed marriage, the million-dollar offer, the entire plan designed to deceive him out of his inheritance. She opened her mouth.

"I know," Colin said.

Her mouth stayed open, but the words she had so

carefully chosen stayed inside her, stuck halfway between her heart and her head.

"I know all about Vivian's plan."

"Everything?" Her lips felt thick and rubbery as if laced with Novocain.

"You're to be a July bride—or, perhaps, August—it's not really important as long as it's soon as possible without arousing suspicion. Hopefully you'll be pregnant by the time you return from the honeymoon. As you said, Hugo wants a new generation. Vivian wants a guarantee Shawn will inherit the estate…and I won't."

He folded his arms and leaned back, giving her a long look. "And you want to join the ranks of envious social stature and unparalleled wealth."

She walked to the window, away from him and his knowing looks. She'd told herself she could take his contempt. She'd been wrong. She stared into the sun. The light was hot, branding.

"Have I left anything out?" he asked behind her.

She closed her eyes, blacking out the sun. "Yes," she answered.

He didn't know everything. She'd come here to tell him the truth, but would he believe her now, after his every suspicion had just been confirmed? He thought she only wanted the money. Could she make him understand all she wanted was to defy her life's legacy?

She could feel the sun's heat through the glass, scalding her skin. Then there was the warm touch of his fingers on her shoulders. She whirled around, opening her eyes, finding him there. His hands remained on her shoulders.

"You're wrong," she told him.

"Am I?" His fingers pressed against her flesh. His eyes were black glass. She saw her own face there and gathered strength.

"Vivian did offer me one million dollars to marry Shawn and have his child."

His fingers tightened. "The part I'm wrong about is…?"

"First I'm to seduce you."

The surprise caught at his features, almost overtook his expression before he gained control of it. Then his gaze steadied, became once more the night.

"Is that what you came here for?"

She tried to step back, break his grip. "I understand your anger."

His hold on her hardened. "You understand nothing."

His features were fixed. His gaze didn't give. She wanted to close her eyes, darkness the only available buffer against the anger, the curses she knew were coming. Her eyes stayed open.

"Vivian said you were desperate for a wife, that you'd be attracted to me to the point where you'd propose," she tried to explain, the words coming too fast. "But on the morning of our wedding day, while you'd be waiting at the altar, I'd be off marrying Shawn, guaranteeing he'd inherit everything."

Colin was still like the eerie calm before a storm.

She didn't move, either, afraid the slightest movement, the shallowest breath would release the fear she felt inside, the fear he wouldn't believe she'd never intended to carry out Vivian's plan.

"You've no feelings for me at all?" he asked.

It wasn't the accusation she'd expected. She didn't know how to answer.

His grip loosened, allowing her to step out of his hold.

"The other night?" he questioned. "That was all part of the setup?"

"No." Her denial was immediate.

"No?" His voice was thick with disbelief.

Aimee sank down on the bench. Haltingly, searching for words that wouldn't be misunderstood, she told him about the boutique closing, the loss of her job, her brother's business battling a larger company.

She didn't tell him about being the unwanted daughter of a whore, the adolescent shuffled through the state system, the young adult who changed her name and came to Newport to forget her past, to begin a new life.

"Vivian told me she was offering me a 'once-in-a-lifetime opportunity,' and I realized she was—an opportunity, for once, not to feel powerless and insignificant, to show her and others like her money can't buy everything…or everyone."

She took a quick breath. "When I made my decision to teach Vivian a lesson, I didn't know about her plan involving you and me."

Colin sat down beside her. "Still you said yes."

"I did," she admitted. "But believe me, I never had any intentions of deceiving you. I had to wait until I had a copy of the signed contract before I could tell you everything. To tell you sooner was too great a risk."

"So you agreed to Vivian's proposal, but never intended to falsely seduce me?"

Aimee studied her newly polished nails. "In the beginning, I thought you could stand to have a bit of the wind let out of your sails."

Colin laughed unexpectedly, the sound lifting, echoing to the rafters. Aimee raised her face to his amused expression.

"That's why you went out with me?"

"No—I mean, yes." The words flew out without thought. She shook her head. "I mean, considering the circumstances..."

A tender smile crossed Colin's face, making Aimee remember the man she'd seen earlier. "I'm glad I'm not the only one confused."

They sat there staring.

"So if you don't intend to deceive me out of my inheritance and marry my half brother, what do you intend to do?"

Aimee outlined her plan. Colin listened, his expression amused.

"There's only one flaw," he commented when she finished.

His index finger touched the back of her hand, then lifted. "I'm attracted to you."

She pulled her hand away.

"Wouldn't it be funny if we really fell in love?" His voice was a silver murmur. "It could happen. Who'd have the last laugh then?"

No, it couldn't happen, Aimee thought with too-quick protest. There'd been too many lies, too many secrets. Even now, she looked at Colin and didn't know which one he was: the cruel one, the content one or the charming one?

"Perhaps my own plan isn't such a good idea after

all.'' She was scared by his attentions, by the rising want inside her.

He leaned toward her. "Are you saying it's over?"

His eyes pulled her to him, his gaze wrapping around her, desire waking.

"It never really began."

He was too close. She tasted his lips before they even found her. Then they touched her as soft as spring rain, tasting smooth, fresh, sweet as ripe fruit warmed by the sun.

They came together, and she met, once more, the man she didn't even know she'd been dreaming of.

The kiss was achingly brief. He pulled away first, but his hand lingered along the side of her face.

"It's begun," he whispered.

She stood up and walked away from him, frightened by the drawing darkness of his eyes. There was the same darkness inside her—a dark, infinite need.

She heard him rise. She felt him coming toward her again. Then she was in his arms again, their bodies fitting together, two halves of one whole. Her hands slid across his shoulders and joined behind his neck. She was suddenly afraid she'd never let him go. Just as quickly she pushed him away.

He wrapped his hand around her wrist as if knowing she was about to bolt. "Let me help you. At least, give me that satisfaction."

His fingers on her skin were warm and comforting, but his expression was cool, composed, waiting for her answer. Once more Aimee had to wonder if he was an ally or an enemy? She had no choice but to find out.

Colin released her arm but offered his hand. "Part-ners?"

She slowly gave him hers. "No more?" she questioned.

"No less," he answered.

He watched her as she walked away. She opened the far door. There was a square of sunlight, then she was gone. He sat down, automatically picking up a piece of wood, but it dangled lifeless in his hands.

Had he only this morning been entertaining thoughts of apology to this woman whose face was so innocent, the lies spun like silver thread off her tongue?

Not that he didn't believe Vivian had hired her to marry Shawn. He'd suspected it long before it'd been confirmed by Aimee's "confession." The scheme to seduce him had been a surprise, but it explained Aimee's attentions and Vivian's approval this past weekend.

It even might've worked, he realized, remembering again his pangs of conscience this morning. Even now, he could taste the raw first taste of vulnerability.

Fortunately Aimee's sudden show of conscience, her assertion to forfeit material gain for a moral aim came before he made a further fool of himself. Alarmed by his suspicions, Vivian must've decided she'd never win…unless Aimee admitted to every-thing, then attempted to secure his sympathies by in-sisting her true aim was to thwart Vivian.

He rubbed the wood in his hands. There was also the possibility Aimee had come to the barn on her own initiative and concocted admirable intentions to protect her own interests. If she played both sides of the battle, it didn't matter who won—she'd be there to share in the spoils. If that was the case, he and Vivian both had underestimated this seeming innocent. Had Vivian met her match? Had he?

What had been lies? What had been truth? Even in his own words, his own profession of feelings, the lines had blurred.

He put down the wood. He couldn't tell anymore in the things she said, in the things he said, where the truth ended and the lies began.

Nor did he know when he'd stopped despising her...

And started to desire her instead.

PAST THE WINDOWS of the office, the sun hovered at the horizon, making way for the moon. Vivian looked up as a new shadow crossed her desk. Colin's figure filled the door frame.

She carefully arranged her expression. "You're back from New York," she said. She didn't invite him in.

He came in nonetheless. "I wasn't sure you knew—"

"Of course I knew."

Colin sat down. "Of course you did." He smiled. She mirrored his smile.

"I owe you an apology."

Vivian folded her hands on top of a stack of invitations. Her artful smile didn't alter.

"I was mistaken about the girl...Aimee," Colin continued. "As you know, we went together to the Preservation Society's fund-raiser the other evening. Now, if she'd been brought here for the reason I imagined—to serve as Shawn's bride—why would she go out with me?''

Vivian's features remained fixed. Colin could see the night coming silent across her face.

''Yes, why would she go out with you?'' she repeated. The shadows lay deeper in the hollows of her cheeks, beneath the shelf of her brow.

He propped his hands on the edge of the desk. ''And why would you seem so…unperturbed about our obvious attraction?'' He paused, allowing the seeds of false security to find soil.

''You like her?'' Vivian asked. The stack of invitations beneath her folded hands flattened, became thin.

He reached for the desk and leaned toward her. ''She's a surprise a minute.'' He watched Vivian's smile almost become real.

He pulled himself up. At the tip of his fingers, a penciled sketch drew his attention. He picked up the loose sheet of paper stacked atop others.

''What's that?'' Vivian demanded, reaching for the paper.

Colin handed her the drawing and looked at the sketch beneath it, then the one beneath that.

''These must be the dresses Aimee's working on for me,'' Vivian said. ''She must've left them on my desk while I was out.''

Colin looked at each one, seeing clothes simple yet stunning, dramatic shapes paired with a soft fluidness. ''They're good,'' he said.

Vivian's head came up. She reached for the others, glancing through them. ''Of course, you're more of an expert than me,'' she began.

"Am I?" he wondered.

She straightened the papers into an even pile. She looked at Colin. "But, you must admit, the girl has many talents."

He feigned a smile. "A surprise a minute."

He turned to leave. Vivian's voice followed him to the door. "Colin, I'm glad you realize Aimee is no more than what she seems. It'll be to everyone's advantage."

He turned. His expression was inscrutable. "Let's hope so."

"GOOD EVENING, everyone," Aimee said.

Vivian looked up. The thin arch of her eyebrows lifted, pulling the skin behind her ears even tighter. Shawn's wineglass, on the way to his mouth, hung midair. Hugo, who'd been speaking, stopped, his mouth open.

Only Colin answered her greeting. "Good evening, Aimee."

She slid into the chair James pulled out for her, and looked around the table, meeting the others' silent stares.

The door to the kitchen swung open, and a girl entered, carrying the first course.

"Great!" Aimee brought her hands together, sounding a single clap. "I'm ready to put on the old feedbag."

"Indeed." Vivian sniffed. "It looks like you already have."

Aimee looked down at her outfit. "Oh, this thing." She smoothed down several bright orange and pink feathers adorning her bosom, but they popped back up like a peacock strutting.

"Please tell me there's a charity costume ball you're attending this evening." Vivian said.

Aimee shook her head, her expression appearing properly confused. "No, I decided I needed a change." She confronted Vivian with a smile as bright as her feathers. "What do you think?"

The other woman's eyes traveled the length of Aimee's sequined, spandexed, feathered torso. Her lips drew in. "I think you've managed to bring together every fashion mistake for the past ten years."

"Vivian," Hugo admonished.

"And what'd you do to your hair?" she demanded, ignoring Hugo.

Aimee gingerly touched the platinum blond spikes on the top of her head. "Just added a few highlights."

"I suppose it could be considered…refreshing," Hugo announced.

"Goodness, don't encourage her," Vivian said.

"I've never seen anything quite like it," Shawn commented.

"I have." Vivian's voice rose. "Call the neighborhood children. The circus has come to town."

"I don't know." Shawn sat back in his chair, sipping from his wineglass, looking at the spiked pouf of Aimee's hair. "It kind of grows on you."

"Like mold," Vivian sputtered.

"Vivian," Hugo warned once more. "Aimee has been brought into this home as a personal assistant. How she chooses to dress in her off hours is none of our business. You only pay her a salary. You don't own her.''

Vivian received his reproach with another lift of her brows.

Aimee shook out her linen napkin with an exaggerated flourish, then tucked it into her feathered cleavage. She turned her attention to the one person who hadn't yet commented. ''What do you think?'' she asked Colin.

''Well...''

Colin's eyes lowered to half-mast, assessing Aimee. She tried not to shift beneath his study, his gaze lazily, seductively moving across her. ''I'd say...as a person hoping for a career in the fashion industry, you're obligated to stay on top of the current trends. I imagine you're also expected to cultivate your own signature.''

He spoke slowly, choosing his words carefully. ''And I think you've certainly accomplished that on both counts.''

Still taking her in, he nodded his head. ''Yes, you've definitely hit the vanguard of the fashion front.''

''Well put,'' Hugo approved.

''Thank you,'' Aimee told Colin. ''I'm glad there's at least one person here who can appreciate what I'm trying to accomplish.''

She unzipped the studded leather fanny pack slung low on her waist and removed a gold compact overrun with rhinestones. She applied an unnecessary layer of fuchsia lipstick to her already-too-bright mouth.

''Is that a nose ring?'' Vivian cried, horrified as a

tiny gold circle in Aimee's nostril caught the light reflected from the compact mirror.

Aimee turned her way.

"Now I'm nauseous." Vivian threw her napkin on the table. "I'll just have dry toast and tea in my bedroom," she instructed the girl serving.

Aimee watched Vivian rise and walk stiffly out of the room. "Hey, Viv, can I have your portion?" she said. "I'm so hungry, I could eat a whole hog—even if it was covered in that black fungus you people favor."

There was a sound like a choked yelp as Vivian walked out the door.

Aimee turned her gaze, inadvertently meeting Colin's eyes. They were smiling, beautiful, big cookie rounds of delight. Her head went light; her stomach felt fluttery as if she was going up in an elevator too fast. The roof of her mouth went dry.

Shawn spoke, and Aimee turned to him, grateful for the diversion. "My friend has been after me to make an appearance at his new club on the wharf. Want to come? He'd probably love something to get people talking."

Before she could answer, Colin cut in, bringing her gaze back to him. "If you prefer, I'm going for a walk along the bluffs after dinner. You could join me." His eyes were still smiling at her.

"She's got on her dancing shoes, not her tennies," Shawn told his half brother.

Aimee looked from one to the other. Although she'd prefer the beach, the opportunity for public display was too perfect. She crossed her fingers, hoping Colin would understand.

"Actually I haven't been clubbing in ages."

She saw the tiniest twitch at the corner of Colin's mouth, but his eyes didn't stop smiling. "Then, do you mind if I join you?" He directed the question to her, ignoring Shawn.

"Three's a crowd," Shawn said.

He wants to help, Aimee told herself, remembering his words this afternoon. She also remembered his touch, his kiss. The attraction pulled deep inside her, threatening to submerge her. She should tell him no. He could flatter her, express feelings for her, but bottom line, he needed a wife. How could she ever believe the words he spoke?

She had to tell him no. The less time together, the less trouble.

She looked up into his eyes. She was lost. "The more, the merrier," she said.

Chapter Six

"You didn't really pierce your nose, did you?" Colin asked.

"What?" Aimee cupped her ear.

He moved closer. "I said you didn't really pierce your nose?"

She smiled and removed the tiny gold ring, revealing its spring clip. "It's a fake." She slipped it into her fanny pack.

He smiled. "Well, it certainly gave Vivian a fright."

"Wait until she sees my tattoo."

Colin's smile became laughter. "You're enjoying yourself, aren't you?"

She looked around the crowded room, still hearing the song of his laugh. "A little."

"A lot." His mouth was still close to her ear. She could feel only his breath on her neck.

"There's a table. Let's grab it," she suggested, moving away.

Still, he took her arm as they maneuvered through the press of people to a small, round table in the corner. She sat down. Colin remained standing.

"I'm going to the bar. Would you like another?" He nodded toward her almost-full glass of chardonnay.

She shook her head no.

"Something else perhaps?"

"No, thank you. I'm fine."

She watched him walk away. She recognized the regal posture, the hard, strong line of his shoulders that rarely softened. From the back, he was the same, but when he faced her, she sometimes saw a change, an accessibility that wasn't there before. Or had she put it there, imagining it like a teenage girl drawing her dream lover?

Was she falling in love with him? she wondered. Or was he falling in love with her? Were the feelings he expressed more than the words of a man who wanted a wife?

The answer didn't really matter. Because a relationship between herself and Colin could never be. Their partnership had begun with secrets and lies; it was being nurtured through deception and dress up, people pretending to be other than what they were. It was far from the formula for happily ever after.

She took a sip of chardonnay. They each had their agenda. Falling in love wasn't on the list. She rested her chin between her hands and pressed her fingers against her temples, trying to focus on her master plan. But she had an awful headache. Her eyes burned from the cigarette smoke. When she took her hands away from her cheeks, her palms were stained with makeup.

COLIN STOOD at the far end of the bar, one foot propped on a brass railing. He stared at Aimee's platinum pouf of hair, her heavy makeup, the clashing colors of her clothes. Beneath the too-bright, too-tight covering, there were curves revealed, their sparkling dip and wave mesmerizing. Then there were those legs, too long in patterned hot pink tights, leading to a skirt of minimum length and metallic material that made a sound when Aimee walked, like the jingle of coins in a lucky gambler's pocket.

Colin reached inside the breast pocket of his jacket and took out a folded sheet of paper. He opened it and looked at the sketch he'd asked Vivian for earlier this evening. It was one of Aimee's drawings—a simple dress, clean and singularly spectacular. He glanced up and saw her once more posed as the perfect candidate for Mr. Blackwell's Worst-Dressed List. He folded the paper, returning it to his pocket. He could feel its heavy bond touch his chest. The girl was far from what she seemed. Any man would be a fool to think otherwise.

AIMEE WIPED her hands on a cocktail napkin, then crumpled it into a ball. She looked around for Colin.

"Have you been abandoned?" Shawn asked, sliding into the chair next to her. He himself had been nowhere to be seen for over an hour. "I thought bright plumage was nature's way of attracting the opposite sex." His gaze skimmed her body.

"I think that only works with birds. Just pray there's no low-flying seagulls along the Avenue."

Shawn laughed his easy laugh and touched his drink glass to hers. "You know, being married to you might not be half-bad."

She heard the slight slur in his words. His rare features were softened by Scotch, previewing what age and drink would do to this man in later years.

"You don't have to sweet-talk me, Shawn." She patted his hand. "I'm already on your side."

He leaned forward, openmouthed, but she averted her head so that the wet kiss landed on her cheek.

Shawn leaned back in his chair, bringing his drink to his mouth. "I see…" He took a slow, long sip, eyeing her. "Saving yourself for the wedding night?" The gleam in his eye was dulled by too much drink.

She looked around the room for Colin, relieved when she finally spied him at the end of the bar. He started back toward the table when a tall redhead touched his arm. They began to talk, the woman keeping her hand on his arm. She said something, and Colin nodded and smiled down at her as though they were sharing a private joke.

Good, Aimee thought, *another woman, another candidate for a wife.* But that wasn't the reaction deep down inside her. There, pangs of jealousy pulsed. She watched him take the woman's hand in both of his as they said goodbye. Aimee looked away.

"Wasn't that Pauline?" Shawn asked when Colin finally reached them.

A swift glance at Aimee, then Colin nodded.

"She's back in town?" Shawn swirled the ice in his drink, his gaze on the redhead.

"Her marriage broke up."

"Is that a fact?" Shawn appraised the statuesque woman.

"The divorce papers were signed last week."

"Pity. Still, our girl looks none the worse for wear."

Shawn's stare shifted to Colin. "I'll bet she was surprised to run into you."

Shawn moved his chair closer to Aimee as if a confidant. "Pauline and Colin were quite an item years ago," he informed. "That is until she met that sheikh—what was he in? Oil? Gas?"

"Both, I imagine," Colin noted dryly.

"Well, whatever it was, he had a title, too. Prince or sultan or swami?" Shawn eyed Colin. "I don't suppose you remember that, either?"

"No." Colin's eyes, midnight without stars, bored into the other man.

"Anyhow," Shawn continued with a wave of his hand, "Pauline always had a thing for royalty, so off she goes with her new title and her old money, leaving our boy here in the lurch."

Aimee saw the sharp edge of Colin's chin. Was it anger at Shawn or feelings for Pauline still so strong that clamped his jaw into a tight line?

Shawn raised his glass. "Here's to Pauline." His gaze crossed the room. Aimee followed his look and saw the other woman, her head thrown back in laughter, the muted lights burnishing the copper glints in her hair. "Divorce certainly hasn't dulled our dear girl."

"Did you ever consider this may be a painful time for her?" Colin asked.

"What's the big deal?" Shawn's gaze glided to his half brother. He took a sip of Scotch. "She gets to keep the title, doesn't she?"

"Maybe," Colin suggested in a low, controlled voice, "she married for more than a title?"

"Oh, sure, it was all for love." Shawn rolled his eyes. "Lovely sentiment."

Colin looked at him. "You talk as though she dumped you."

"No, little brother." Shawn took a sip of his drink, a smile just visible above the rim of the glass. "She dumped you."

Colin's face whitened with anger. The black fury in his eyes shone in cold contrast. "So you keep reminding me."

The smirk left Shawn's face as if he realized he'd gone too far. Still, the Scotch spoke. "Perhaps other people can afford to marry for love, but not the people in our world. There's too much at stake. Anyone who thinks otherwise is a fool."

Colin stood, giving Shawn one final cutting look, but when he turned to Aimee, she saw only tiredness. "If you're ready, I'll take you home."

"You don't want to leave yet," Shawn insisted. "The fun is just beginning." He reached for her knee. She shifted her legs to the opposite side of the chair.

"I've had my share of fun for the night," Colin said to her. "But if you're not tired yet, that walk can still be arranged."

Aimee fingered an orange feather. She looked up at Colin above her, feeling defenseless against the dark beckoning in his eyes. He didn't even have to ask, she realized. She'd been his since the first night, since the first moment she turned to him and the rest of the world fell away. She knew now, it was that fear that had pulled her hand away, forced her back. It was the same fear now that told her to refuse him, take a cab back to sleep a sleepless night and cry a virgin's soundless cries.

The embers of anger in his eyes were cooling. If she turned him down again, the second time that night, surely his anger would flare once more. Deny him twice, and his confessed feelings for her, whether real or only of necessity, would begin to waver, even dissolve.

She looked up into his face, and the answer was already spoken. "Actually, a little sea air is exactly what I need right now."

Above her, a smile spread across Colin's lips. He reached out his hand for her and, for a mad moment, it didn't matter what had come before, what would come after. All that mattered was this man.

THE NEXT MORNING, the door to Aimee's bedroom swung open. There was no knock. Aimee, sitting at the vanity, looked into the mirror and saw her intended mother-in-law in riding gear.

Aimee continued blending turquoise eye shadow up to her brow. "Going for a ride, Vivian?"

"I'm already being taken for one."

She strode into the room, the riding crop in her hand marking each step. Her controlled expression gave way, unmasking her anger. She stopped in the middle of the room. "I wasn't impressed by your little performance last evening."

Aimee reached for a silver tube and slowly unscrewed it. "As I remember, you seemed quite affected."

The crop continued to keep a beat against Vivian's thigh. "What is that hideous thing you've got on now?" she demanded.

Aimee splayed her hand across a lime-green yoke. "It's a muumuu, Mama."

Vivian reached for the bedpost to steady herself. Her diaphragm lifted, then released as she took a deep breath. Still using the bedpost for support, she sat on the edge of the bed. The tight strap beneath her chin pulled her features into restraint. She crossed her legs, her breeches swelling above the knee, slim below. Her crop tapped the inseam of her booted ankle. "Your family doesn't have a history of mental illness, do they?"

Aimee laughed, the line she was drawing on her lips going crooked. "Not that I'm aware, but…" She twisted on the stool, the face she turned toward Vivian serious except for a magenta zigzag across her mouth. "All those years of inbreeding had to show up sooner or later."

Vivian's lips tightened, became a colorless ring. "You find this amusing?"

Aimee had turned back to the mirror and was wiping the lip color off with a tissue. "You want to have me committed because I'm developing my own signature style? Since when did individuality become part of the insanity defense?"

The crop tapped faster, its tabbed end spinning. "Don't give me that nonsense about making a fashion statement. The only designer I know that would find you charming would be Frederick's of Hollywood. Is that what you're aspiring to? A career in peekaboo bras?"

"I think the real money's in thong underwear."

The crop stopped. Vivian's entire body went still except for a pulsing flare of her nostrils. "There's a difference between personal style and looking like a poster child for bad taste. Take my advice, dressing like the village idiot isn't the way to Colin's heart."

Aimee licked her lips and began to reapply color. "I didn't realize it was his heart you'd hired me to attract."

There was a quick cluck from Vivian. "Just because you look vulgar, doesn't mean you have to act it."

Aimee looked into the mirror's reflection and caught Vivian's glare. "What's vulgar, Vivian, is offering someone a million dollars to marry your son." She returned to lining her lips. "I'm only giving you what you paid for."

"I see." Vivian's features turned glassy. She stood and walked to where Aimee sat. Aimee could smell a subtle blend of flowers. Vivian placed her hands on Aimee's shoulders. Her touch was dry, bloodless.

"So far, what I've paid is nothing," she said.

She leaned down, bringing her image beside Aimee's in the mirror. "And it looks like I got what I paid for." Her hold tightened on Aimee's shoulders. "A nothing who could've been something."

Aimee's hand was still poised with the fine-haired lip brush. She laid it flat as it started to tremble. She covered it with her other hand. She stared back at Vivian's reflection.

Vivian straightened. Her hands fell from Aimee's shoulders. "Obviously I've made a mistake."

Aimee turned and faced her. "What's your mistake?"

The crop hit once against Vivian's jodhpured thigh. "My mistake was offering someone like you my generosity and expecting gratitude."

Aimee wagged an index finger at her. "You're catching on...but no cigar."

Vivian looked down at her. "Perhaps you'd care to enlighten me?"

"Nope." Aimee swung back around to the mirror. "This is a lesson you've got to learn for yourself."

"No," Vivian disagreed. "I've learned all the lessons I need to learn. I'll expect you out of here before I return for lunch."

Aimee choose a violet eyeliner from the vanity table. "Too late."

"Too late?"

Aimee leaned close to the mirror and applied a sharp line of color beneath her lower lashes. "We've an agreement. An agreement I'm prepared to share with the world."

"You wouldn't dare."

Aimee's reflection smiled up at the other woman. "You've already made one mistake. Don't make another."

Vivian's features, strapped in black and crowned by the hard brim of her riding helmet, went rigid. Her hand holding the crop tightened. The blue veins along the back of her hand bulged.

She turned and marched toward the door, the crop's tabbed end making little whipping sounds. Aimee waited until she got to the doorway.

"Vivian." She stopped her.

The other woman looked back at her.

"Hope you enjoy your ride."

The bedroom door slammed. A lipstick toppled from the vanity and rolled onto the floor.

"Round one," Aimee said to her own reflection. She leaned over to pick up the lipstick, grasping the tube tightly to still the shiver in her hand. The tremor moved upward along her arm, gathering strength.

She turned away from the mirror and went to the window, trying to still her emotions. She saw the winding route below the avenue, the hills steep and dressed with wildflowers. It was there Colin and she had walked last night. They'd walked a long time, his controlled expressions no longer visible in the darkness, her garishly drawn face dissolved by the night.

But when they'd returned to the estate, their goodnights became as self-conscious as their grand surroundings. She'd gone straight to bed, clasping her hands beneath her cheek and curling her body as if it'd gone back to the womb. Still, sleep wouldn't come. So in the quiet hours between midnight and morning, she'd found herself out on the front steps, a glittering incongruity between alabaster pillars. There she'd sat, waiting for the sunrise to bring color to the surrounding gloom, for the warm oranges, pinks and reds to reflect off her own costumed bosom.

She sat back down at the vanity. In the bright light of day, she looked into the mirror and saw the colored lines of her face blurring, felt the involuntary quiver of her muscles. And knew the cause was more than insomnia and Vivian with her Eden of material riches.

It was Colin.

She felt it in every breath she took. Desire. Complete chaos of the body. It was the sound of doors opening and windows rising. She felt air and openness and freedom rushing in.

And it terrorized her. Vivian's lure of moneyed privilege she could fight, even parody with her own rhinestoned, neoned caricature.

She had no defenses against this attraction to Colin. At their first meeting, when her hand pulled back and her body had stepped away, she should've listened to her instinct signaling flight.

Now she had to fight.

She would dress, become what she was not. She would smile and prance. Her alter ego had been born for Vivian's benefit, but it would now serve double-duty as a whimsical camouflage of any feelings.

She completed the paint-by-numbers finish of her face and went to the closet. She looked at the clothes of her own design, touching their subtle shades and elegant lines, but chose instead a ruffled, midriff-baring top in red bandanna print and a pair of denim hot pants studded at the seams. She teased her hair up into a high bouffant, then weaved two braids at the nape of her neck. She selected big, red plastic hoops to dangle from her ears and a string of red beads to wrap around her bare waist. She slipped her feet into clear plastic open-toed heels and spun once in front of the bureau mirror for the full effect.

"Elly Mae, eat your heart out," she said to the reflection. Head high, arms lifted for counterbalance and with a wiggle only possible in plastic high heels, Aimee stepped out of the room.

She was pouring herself a cup of coffee in the kitchen when James found her.

"Good morning." His professional reserve allowed no more than a quick crinkle at the corner of his eyes as he looked at her. He handed her a piece of paper. "Before Mrs. Tremont left, she asked me to give you this list of errands."

Aimee scanned the paper, then folded it and put it in the back pocket of her tight shorts. She smiled at James, offering him the cup of coffee in her hands. After she poured herself another, they headed toward the long stainless-steel table in the center of the room.

"Awful hectic in here this morning," she noted, sidestepping a boy carrying a tray full of glasses. "What's the big scooby-doo?"

James took a sip of coffee. "The ladies of the Historical Society are coming for lunch and to plan their annual charity fashion show."

Aimee looked up over the rim of her coffee cup. "You don't say?"

James stirred his coffee. "Very old guard. You practically have to be born into the organization to become a member. Strictly protocol all the way."

Aimee set down her coffee cup. "Do tell."

"Why, even Mrs. Tremont campaigned like a common cottager before they accepted her application. Of course, that was after she showed her generous financial support of their organization."

Aimee twirled the end of one of her braids. "And they're coming here today?"

James nodded. "Mrs. Tremont's first luncheon for the society. Tables and chairs are being set up on the back grounds now."

"Mmm-mmm-mmm, I'd hate to miss Mrs. Tremont's first luncheon for the society. It must be awful important to her."

James sipped his coffee and nodded in agreement.

Aimee pulled the piece of paper from her back pocket. "But it looks as if she's determined to keep me busy all day today."

James reached for the paper and looked it over. "This is an awful long list."

"Yes," Aimee agreed. "Excessively long, wouldn't you say?"

James nodded, his professional poker face never altering. "Almost as if she wanted you out of the house for some reason."

"Can you imagine?" Aimee put her hands on her hips. "And here I thought we were beginning to bond."

She succeeded in mustering a faint smile from James.

He tore the bottom half of the list and handed the top part back to Aimee. "I'm certain I can find someone to help you with all these errands."

"Thank you, James." Aimee leaned over and kissed the old man's cheek.

"Now, now." He waved away her gratitude. "You just make sure you do your share."

Aimee smiled. "What time is lunch?"

SHE LAY beneath the trimmed yew, listening to well-modulated female voices and the occasional lilt of discreet laughter. Then there was the sound of Vivian's voice rising above the others with a welcoming "Ladies…"

"Show time," Aimee whispered. She sat up, stretching so her arms reached above the yew. Then she rose, naked except for a tattooed dancing duck on her backside. Beneath the duck it read Born To Boogie. Trailing a towel, she started to cross the lawn toward the house.

She heard the gasps and exclamations, at first sparse, then rising, but she didn't stop until she heard Vivian's "God preserve me."

Aimee turned toward the crowd, feigning surprise. Expressions of shock came at her like a sharp wave.

"I'm sorry. I didn't mean to disturb your gathering." Her arms opened in a generous expanse. "Please, continue."

Vivian was marching toward her.

"Gorgeous day for sunbathing, but I don't want to get too much of a good thing."

She saw Vivian snatch a napkin out of the hand of a woman in a large straw hat brimmed with white magnolias.

"You know how those sensitive spots burn, ladies."

Another woman offered Vivian her napkin as she passed. She came toward Aimee, flapping the napkins as if signaling a seagull for landing.

"Cover yourself," she hissed. She started to put the napkins up to Aimee's chest, hesitated, lowered them to hip level, hesitated again. Completely at a loss, she shoved them at Aimee. "You do it."

Aimee accepted the napkins, gracefully shook one

out and patted a tiny bead of sweat above Vivian's upper lip. Vivian's head reared back.

Aimee patted the back of her own neck, stretching her arm, lifting her rib cage. "Things are heating up, aren't they, Vivian?"

"Get some clothes on now." Vivian's voice was no more than a rasp.

Aimee smiled. "But Vivvie, I thought you didn't like my wardrobe?"

"Go," Vivian commanded.

"Aren't you going to introduce me?"

"Go."

"That's rather rude, isn't it?" Aimee leaned past Vivian's shoulder and waved at the other ladies. "Everyone, I'm Vivian's new personal assistant."

"Go," Vivian said again, her voice raw with rage.

"Okay, okay." Aimee held up a placating hand. "I can see you're about to go for a shrimp fork."

She turned her Born To Boogie inscribed backside to the crowd and sauntered toward the house. She glanced once over her shoulder. Vivian was walking back toward the tables with a slow, stiff gait. A woman in an apricot pillbox hat reached out and took Vivian's hand, stopping her.

"She's French, isn't she?" the woman asked.

Chapter Seven

Aimee headed up the street toward the wharves, avoiding the glances of the scrubbed sailors from the naval complex and the eager-faced young men down from Brown, working as waiters, bartenders, and tour guides for the summer.

She stopped at the corner, in front of a building for rent, and watched for Jack. Soon, however, the building's wide, empty windows drew her. She stood, nose to glass, and saw inside walls of black-and-white tile perfect to provide crisp contrast for her clothes of subdued colors, relaxed lines. The store's ceiling was low; the room narrow, small and, besides the tiled walls, nondescript. Yet Aimee saw a flawless, tiny showcase for fabric spun into fantasy.

She stepped back. The dream faded. Left was only her own image in the empty window.

"Aimee." She heard Jack's call. She turned, scanning the parade of people until she found him. He came toward her, his eyes focused on her, dark with concern.

"Jack," she answered, throwing her arms around him as he reached her. They held on tight for several minutes. Their arms stayed linked as they started down the street.

They stopped at a tavern looking out to the sea, and sat down, looking at each other across the table, the thick accents of Portuguese and Greek fishermen surrounding them.

As Jack started to talk, Aimee did, too. They both stopped and laughed, looking at each other. It hadn't been many days, but it was the first time since they'd been reunited as adults that they'd been apart.

"Come home," he said to her now.

Past Jack's shoulder, Aimee could see the large sign heralding the future home of the Tremont mall. She looked back into the eyes of her brother and saw the only unconditional love she'd ever known. She laid her hand on his.

"Soon." She saw a frown appear between his brows. The dark circles beneath his eyes had deepened since the last time she saw him.

"How's business?" she asked.

He slid his hand out from beneath hers. "We'll get by."

We'll get by. It'd always been Jack's motto, even before Nana had died, even before their mother's drug overdose, even when the state had separated them, sending Jack, angry and defiant, to an institution for troubled boys. Aimee had gone to an orphanage where the nuns had taught her to sew, then to a series of foster homes. But on the day she "aged out," Jack had been there, waiting for her. He'd brought her to Newport. *They'd gotten by.*

"How's your 'business'?" he asked, reaching for the mug of beer the waitress sat before him.

Her hands rounded her own cool glass. "I don't want to just get by anymore." The words startled her as much as Jack.

He pushed back from the table and looked at her. "What're you trying to tell me? You're taking the money and marrying a damn Tremont?"

"No, never." Her answer was immediate and adamant.

Jack pushed away the platter of cheeseburger and fries the waitress set down. His hands on the table rolled into fists.

"Then what're you saying?"

"I'm trying to explain, trying to make you understand why I accepted Vivian Tremont's offer."

She told him about the feelings of powerlessness, shame, frustration aroused by Vivian's offer. She tried to describe the moment when she'd decided to show Vivian she wasn't an object, she was a human being.

She told him the highlights of the past few days—the contract, the costumes, the scene in front of the Historical Society. The only part she left out was her confusing attraction to Colin, certain the less said about her feelings for him, the easier their existence could be denied.

Smiling, her brother shook his head. "You streaked across the Tremont's back grounds?"

"I didn't streak. I'd say I sauntered my rear across their rear."

Jack let out full laughter. He lifted the hem of his T-shirt and wiped his eyes. "I'll bet Vivian Tremont will think twice before she offers someone a million dollars again."

Aimee reached for a fry and bit it in half. "Exactly."

"Now you've had your fun. You've made your point." Her brother picked up his cheeseburger in one calloused hand. "Come home."

She looked at him. "But I've only begun to bring new definition to the term *bad taste*."

Jack took a big bite of his burger. Chewing, he said, "You've made your impression."

Aimee looked down at her uneaten meal.

"Now it's over," Jack said.

She looked up and met her brother's gaze. "It's only beginning. I've got a lot more planned than a little indecent exposure before the Historical Society."

Jack pointed a French fry at her. "How far are you going with this?"

"All the way."

"All the way to what?" Jack shook his head. "You think you can make these people care about you, about anyone but themselves?"

Aimee looked down at her cold food.

"I don't want to see you get hurt, sis."

"I don't intend to get hurt."

"Nobody intends to get hurt."

She looked up. "Don't worry." She smiled and touched her brother's wide hand. "I've got it all under control."

But even as she said the words, she knew her feelings for Colin threatened, dammed only by the feeble voice of her denial.

Was it too late? Had the feelings grown, deepened,

become unwieldy? In this fool's pantomime, had she fallen in love with him?

"Mom's dead, Aimee." Jack abruptly interrupted her thoughts. "You can't get her attention anymore. You can't prove anything to her."

"You think… That's not… Where did you…?" She fell silent, unable to tell him he was wrong. After all, he'd been there, too, beside her in the world where children didn't belong. She bowed her head away from his tender stare.

He reached over and took her hand. "You're much more than another one of Mom's mistakes. Don't you ever think otherwise. You don't have to prove that to anyone."

She looked up at him. "Yes, I do. I have to prove it to myself."

It was late when Jack dropped her off. She watched until the van's red lights disappeared in the darkness, then she turned to the house. It loomed large and black, its windows dark, shuttered with secrets. She let herself in through the back and padded silently through the kitchen, grateful the others were either out or asleep.

The stairs were in her sight when, passing by one of the many rooms lining the hall, she heard Colin's voice.

"We missed you at dinner."

She stopped, wondering if she'd only imagined it, if her suffering heart had invented the words and the mild coax of his voice? She could continue on, pretend she hadn't heard. She could slip up the stairs and, within seconds, slide between the bedclothes, soliciting sleep's oblivion.

She saw his shadow, then Colin himself in the doorway, backlit by the room's muted light. Any thoughts of escape fled.

"Come." He gestured with the snifter of amber liquid he held. "It's been a long day. I've missed you. Come have a nightcap with me."

He only had to say "Come," and her steps started his way. She stopped in the doorway, fashioning her features into a detached pose. There was still time. If she could turn around now, deny his invitation, she'd be safe.

COLIN LOOKED AT HER, standing in the doorway, the darkness behind her. The fire from the far wall lit her hair, her skin, turned the white cotton of her T-shirt luminescent. A shimmering blade of a woman. She was centered in the entry, not veering to the left or the right, not seeking the support of the doorjamb. She paused, surveying the room as if it were her kingdom, and he her fortunate subject.

He went to her, beside her before she could step back. She looked at him, and all impervious tilt to her features left. Her lips parted, and she became a mere mortal after all, a woman in love.

No, Colin told himself. He was only projecting his own desire, superimposing his need. He looked at her and saw a song sung from the beginning of time. She was young, but in those eyes, those lips, the incomplete curve of her cheek was the ageless face of the sweet temptress. The innocent above, the corrupter beneath, sent to cajole, coax, then crucify her prey.

Still he wanted her. He wanted her like nothing else before or to come. Even convinced the flush of innocence was a façade and those virginal lips hungered for far more than the taste of him, he wanted this sweet siren in his bed.

He felt the contempt come, turn inward. He was the fool. He knew exactly what she was, what she wanted, and he wanted her all the more. Perhaps his father had been blinded, but he had no such excuse. His eyes were open, and still he sought his own destruction. For destroy him she would, with no more than one kiss from those childlike lips.

He took her hand and led her to the settee. "Where are your glad rags?" he asked, turning his back to her and going to the row of crystal decanters on the sideboard.

He poured her a drink, refreshed his own and turned back to her. "No boas or bangles this evening?" He handed her a rounded goblet. Smiling, he sat down beside her.

Her hands cupped the brandy snifter. She slowly swirled the large glass, its liquid catching firelight. "I know it looks easy, but it's hard work being trashy."

Colin smiled, tasted his cognac. "So you took the day off?"

"Not the day, just the night." She took a sip of the brandy. It bit at the tip of her tongue, then slid down her throat as if seeking empty areas inside her.

"Really?" Colin opened the carved humidor on the coffee table and selected a long cigar almost as slim as a cigarette. He held it beneath his nostrils, his nose following the length of it, his eyes closing for a moment. He brought the thin cigar to his lips and lit it, puffing softly. "You worked hard today then?" He exhaled a silver stream of smoke.

The smoke mingled with the summoning scent of the cognac. She raised her oversize glass and inhaled.

"I once read on a fortune cookie that if you enjoy what you do, you'll never work another day in your life."

He inhaled, eyeing her. The thin cigar was clamped between his teeth. "You enjoy what you do?"

"Do you?" she challenged.

"Do I?" He leaned forward, setting the cigar on a brass ashtray. "I'm not sure I find it as infinitely entertaining as your current calling."

"Hugo said you work like a fiend."

"Yes, I remember."

"Why?"

He leaned back and looked at her, his expression faintly amused. "Why?" There was further amusement in his voice.

"Yes, why?"

"An old politician friend of mine in New York taught me words to live by several years ago. Never Complain Or Explain."

Her hand reached out as if she was going to touch him.

"You don't have to prove anything to anyone." She repeated the words her brother had said to her only hours ago.

Her hand hovered, then stopped, fell to the properly aged tapestry of the cushion. Still, Colin looked as if she might have touched him.

He picked up the cigar and placed it between his lips, giving her only his profile. "Tell me about your day," he said.

Her hand lifted and went back to her lap. "This afternoon I walked naked through Vivian's luncheon for the Historical Society."

He looked at her now, his eyes contracting into a squint. "Naked?"

"Except for a duck temporarily tattooed on my butt proclaiming Born To Boogie."

He puffed on the cigar, his eyes narrowing. "You mooned the Historical Society?"

She nodded.

The cigar still tight between his teeth, he leaned his head back, and rich laughter like the sea's waves at high tide spilled out of him.

He should always laugh like that, Aimee thought, his joyful abandon releasing the hard lines of his face, warming the cool center of his eyes. The deep sound of his amusement spun and settled on her softly. Gradually everything in the room—the warmth of the fire, the fluid shadows in the cognac, the simple lay of her shirt against her skin—seemed soft, yielding. Colin's laughter wrapped around her, and she sat, so embraced.

He removed his cigar, resting it on the ashtray's shiny surface. Pleasure still dominated his features, parting his mouth, releasing a warmth and accessibility that made Aimee want to bring her mouth down on those open, laughing lips and taste his joy.

"That explains Vivian's odd behavior this evening," he said, his eyes still alive with amusement. "When Hugo asked at dinner how the Historical So-

ciety luncheon went, she nearly choked on the rad-
icchio. James was called in to give her the Heim-
lich.''

"Oh, no." Aimee's hand covered her mouth.

"Don't worry." He touched the back of her hand
once lightly. "It was far from serious. This family is
famous for its melodramatic dinners. Shawn didn't
even look up from his salad except to ask the girl
serving for a splash more raspberry vinaigrette."

Aimee's hand came away from her mouth. "She
was okay?"

"Vivian always survives…and in high style," he
reassured her. "Although I wouldn't put it past her
to fake her own death to wriggle out of this gaffe. I
can see her tombstone now. Felled By A Faux Pas."

She looked at him alarmed. "You're not serious."

"No." He touched the back of her hand once
more. "But you certainly are, to show the Historical
Society your dancing duck."

She smiled. "One lady kept chugging water until
she'd emptied everyone's glass on the table. Colin,
you should've seen it."

"I wish I had, my love."

The endearment took away Aimee's ease, reminded her of her own vulnerability whenever she
was too near this man. She set down her drink and
pressed her hands against the couch as if preparing
to rise. "So Vivian's okay?"

"It isn't the first time her reputation has almost
been ruined," Colin noted. "In fact, she recovered
sufficiently enough to take Shawn and I to task about
the blurb in Cecilia's column—"

"Cecilia?"

"Cecilia Rathmore," he explained. "She has that column in *The New News*—'Cecilia Sez.' Normally she covers New York, but summertime, when everyone who's anyone leaves the city, she flits around the hangouts of the rich and ridiculous—the Hamptons, Saratoga, Newport, the Vineyard. Vivian and her gang detest her, whisper she's a *bottom feeder*. They've an unwritten rule she isn't allowed at any of the invitation-only social events."

"Then she couldn't have been at the luncheon this afternoon."

"No, but she was at Shawn's friend's club last night."

Understanding swept across Aimee's features. "Oopsie." Her lips puckered. Her eyes took on a Betty Boop wideness.

"There was a picture heading her column today of you, smiling and feathered, looking like a peacock on Prozac. Shawn and I were on either side of you. The caption began Ménage A Millionaires, and wondered if the Tremont brothers had found the lost link between fun and a summer spent in Newport. It was definitely one for your scrapbook."

"First the column, followed by the luncheon," Aimee mused.

"Yes." Colin smiled. "You have been a busy bee. No wonder Vivian suggested I take you back to New York with me tomorrow."

"New York?"

He nodded. "Since she's having you coordinate all the arrangements for the benefit fashion show—"

"What?"

Colin eyed her. "You didn't know?"

Aimee let out a short laugh. "After this afternoon, the only thing I thought she'd have me coordinate was my funeral arrangements."

"She said it would be a perfect platform for your introduction into the worlds of both fashion and society." Colin leaned in close. "But I think you've already taken care of your society debut."

She looked into his eyes. "New York?"

"Have you ever been?"

She shook her head. "I've never really been anywhere."

"Then you must come. Leonard's has a business suite at the Plaza. You'll stay there."

"The Plaza?"

"You can tour Leonard's, meet with our general merchandise manager, talk to the head buyers for women's wear. You'll want to see the garment district. We can arrange some personal tours of the designer houses. I know you must love Agnes B. Did you know she has a boutique in SoHo? Have you seen the Phantom?"

He paused only long enough for Aimee to shake her head.

"You and I are probably the only two people left on the face of the planet who haven't. If I can arrange my workload, maybe we could take it in. And who knows? With all the real celebrities abandoning the city for the summer, we might even find a gossip columnist or two to take our picture and speculate on our relationship. It'll be a working vacation."

He sat back against the sofa. "Plus planning the fashion show will be a wonderful opportunity for you. It'll give you a chance to work with some of the most knowledgeable people in the field. Most important, it'll allow you to show off some of your designs to the toughest but richest critics in the Western hemisphere.''

''My designs?''

''Of course. Vivian's exact words were 'The show will be the perfect launch for my little protégée into the fashion world.' Obviously, she intends to feature your designs.''

''But I don't understand.'' Aimee's voice was still thick with disbelief. ''After the luncheon, you'd think the only thing she'd want to launch of mine would be my luggage onto the front yard.''

''Rest assured Vivian does nothing without good reason,'' He tapped the cigar against the ashtray and brought it back to his mouth. ''My first guess is she's hoping to impart some social standing before you walk down the aisle with her son.''

''But I'm not going—''

He held up a halting hand. ''You know you're not going to marry Shawn, and I know you're not going to marry Shawn, but Vivian doesn't, right?''

''Right,'' she agreed.

He took a final puff on the cigar, then stubbed it out in the ashtray. ''So if you prove yourself an adept fund-raiser, a very important skill among the idle rich, no one may remember you as the girl with the boogie-woogie duck on her backside.''

''You think that's it?''

''My second guess is Vivian's no fool. I've seen some of your designs. They're good.''

''They're good?'' Excitement automatically colored her voice.

"They're good," he repeated for her benefit. "Snag a couple of wealthy clients at this show, and who knows where it'll lead."

She couldn't sit still. She had to stand up and take several turns around the room.

From the sofa, watching her, Colin said, "My third guess is Vivian knows in New York you can be outlandish as you please, and the worst that can happen is they'll ignore you. What's more likely to happen is you'll start a new trend.

"My fourth and final guess is Vivian wants you out of town when *Lifestyle* comes next week and does its article on 'The Belles of Bellevue Avenue.'"

"*Lifestyle* magazine? They're doing an article on Newport?"

"Not all of Newport. Just the part *Lifestyle* and its readers thinks is important."

"And Vivian knows about the article?"

Colin took a sip of cognac. "She's practically frothing at the mouth."

"But you said she didn't like publicity." She walked back to the sofa and sat down.

"She doesn't like *crass* publicity, but, among her crowd, to be featured among the pages of *Lifestyle* magazine is a real coup."

He drank the last of his cognac and set down the glass. "After today's exhibition, Vivian obviously wants you out of the way when the *Lifestyle* people arrive."

He gathered her hand in his so easily. "Don't worry. I wouldn't let you miss an opportunity for national coverage. It may even be the perfect time to announce our engagement."

Play **TIC-TAC-TOE** and get **FREE GIFTS!**

HOW TO PLAY:

1. Play the tic-tac-toe scratch-off game at the right for your FREE BOOKS and FREE GIFT!

2. Send back this card and you'll receive TWO brand-new Harlequin American Romance® novels. These books have a cover price of $3.99 each in the U.S. and $4.50 each in Canada, but they are yours to keep absolutely free.

3. There's no catch. You're under no obligation to buy anything. We charge nothing — ZERO — for your first shipment. And you don't have to make any minimum number of purchases — not even one!

4. The fact is, thousands of readers enjoy receiving books by mail from the Harlequin Reader Service® months before they're available in stores. They like the convenience of home delivery, and they love our discount prices!

5. We hope that after receiving your free books you'll want to remain a subscriber. But the choice is yours — to continue or cancel, any time at all! So why not take us up on our invitation, with no risk of any kind. You'll be glad you did!

YOURS *FREE*

A FABULOUS **MYSTERY GIFT!**

**We can't tell you what it is...
but we're sure you'll like it!**

A FREE GIFT—
just for playing

TIC-TAC-TOE!

DETACH AND MAIL CARD TODAY!

With a coin, scratch the gold boxes on the tic-tac-toe board. Then remove the "X" sticker from the front and affix it so that you get three X's in a row. This means you can get **TWO FREE** Harlequin American Romance® novels and a **FREE MYSTERY GIFT!**

PLAY **TIC-TAC-TOE**

YES! Please send me the 2 Free books and gift for which I qualify. I understand that I am under no obligation to purchase any books, as explained on the back of this card.

354 HDL CX7F

154 HDL CX64
(H-AR-01/00)

Name: _____
(PLEASE PRINT CLEARLY)

Address: _____ Apt.#: _____

City: _____ State/Prov.: _____ Zip/Postal Code: _____

The Harlequin Reader Service® — Here's how it works:

Accepting your 2 free books and gift places you under no obligation to buy anything. You may keep the books and gift and return the shipping statement marked "cancel." If you do not cancel, about a month later we'll send you 4 additional novels and bill you just $3.34 each in the U.S., or $3.71 each in Canada, plus 25¢ delivery per book and applicable taxes if any.* That's the complete price and — compared to the cover price of $3.99 in the U.S. and $4.50 in Canada — it's quite a bargain! You may cancel at any time, but if you choose to continue, every month we'll send you 4 more books, which you may either purchase at the discount price or return to us and cancel your subscription.

*Terms and prices subject to change without notice. Sales tax applicable in N.Y. Canadian residents will be charged applicable provincial taxes and GST.

If offer card is missing write to: Harlequin Reader Service, 3010 Walden Ave., P.O. Box 1867, Buffalo, NY 14240-1867

BUSINESS REPLY MAIL
FIRST-CLASS MAIL   PERMIT NO. 717   BUFFALO, NY

POSTAGE WILL BE PAID BY ADDRESSEE

HARLEQUIN READER SERVICE
3010 WALDEN AVE
PO BOX 1867
BUFFALO NY 14240-9952

NO POSTAGE
NECESSARY
IF MAILED
IN THE
UNITED STATES

She looked up into his eyes, seeing the dark flickers of firelight there. She felt the touch of his hand, their fingers joined like two teen lovers. An ache began within her.

"Of course, the engagement will be a sham, but only you and I will know that."

She should let go of his hand, she told herself. With only a touch he'd taken hostage of her sensibilities, her very reason. What would happen if he came closer? If he kissed her, openmouthed, those sharply drawn lips seeking her, moving down, away from her mouth to her neck, the edge of her collarbone to the peak of her breasts tightening now with no more than the thought.

He held her hand and said, "It'll all be a put-on. Only you and I will know we don't really have feelings for one another."

She looked into those eyes of dark fire. Would they close if he kissed her or remain open, watching her warily?

"I understand," he said suddenly.

She looked at him, for one mad moment, imagining he'd read her thoughts, seen the images she saw even now—his mouth sliding slowly down the stretch of her stomach, nibbling, nipping, moving on, marking a trail with a slow, long sweep of his tongue. Did he see her thighs parting with their own promise, her body lifting, pressing against the moist heat of his mouth, lips, teeth, convulsing with passion as he found the secret ache inside her and subdued it?

"You're frightened of me," he said.

Scared to death.

"Recently I expressed feelings that, perhaps, were

better left unsaid. Feelings I know now you don't
share and can't return,'' he was saying.

All the while she was seeing images of him touching her intimately, she reaching for him, drawing him
down upon her, wrapping her legs around those slim
hips.

''I've accepted this and respect your choice. Don't
be afraid of me. I plan to be a perfect gentleman.''

He lifted her hand, pressing her palm to his chest.
The contact was so unexpected, Aimee didn't have
time to pull away. Beneath her hand, she could feel
the bold pressure of bone, the thick twine of muscle,
the sweet promise of skin. Colin's hand covered her
own, warm and smooth and large.

''Cross my heart,'' he said in a low murmur.

He must've seen the fear in her face. ''Let me
prove it to you.''

His head bent, and his mouth, that mouth of her
wild imaginings, was on hers with a sweet, light,
barest of touches, his lips no more than a maybe
against her, brushing back and forth, savoring her
softness.

He straightened. ''There, you see. I'm not an animal controlled only by base desire. I can kiss you.''

He leaned forward and did it again, so swiftly,
Aimee's lips were still shaped by his touch when he
rested once again against the couch's low back and
looked at her.

''And I enjoy it, yes. But you've made your position more than clear to me. I've resigned myself to
being your friend and appeased myself with the
thought of possibly assisting you in your entertaining
endeavors. I could even kiss you like this....''

He bowed his head to her still-puckered lips and claimed them, opening them as she'd dreamed. He curved his hand to the shape of her neck, supporting her as his tongue pushed itself, full and wet, inside her mouth. His tongue moved, smoothing the inside of her cheeks, stroking the roof of her mouth, teasing the tip of her own tongue until her mouth contracted, sucking the fat, hard length filling her.

Gone was softness and sweetness, and when her chest arched to his, the hard tips of her breasts straining against the fine fabric of his tailored shirt, he obliged. His hand released the length of hair it had knotted in its fist and cupped the pressing curve of her breast, his palm, strong and wide, moving back and forth against the stiff tip.

Her body went soft and surrendered to the stretch of couch beneath her. His mouth stayed hard and hungry on hers. Her arms wrapped around his neck, her thighs opened, embracing him. His other hand abandoned the nape of her neck and found her other breast, caressed it, the heat of his hand felt though the light barrier of cotton and lace. His mouth moved on hers, echoed in the writhing movement of her body. His hands stroked and smoothed, his fingers touched and teased until she groaned into his open mouth and pressed her pelvis to the swell of his desire.

Then, suddenly, she was released. Colin sat up and, not touching her anywhere, turned and looked down at her. She lay, spread before him, the sudden end shocking her senses as much as the sudden start. She could feel her lips thick from his kisses, her hair tangled by his hands, the throb throughout her whole body pulsing, crying out for him.

He offered his hand politely and assisted her into a sitting position.

"You see, I can even kiss you like that," he said, his expression calm, not belying any signs of discomfort or unrequited desire. "Then, stop, shake your hand like a partner..." He took her limp hand and shook it lightly.

"And say good night."

He released her hand. "You see, I'm in complete control of my attraction to you. You've nothing to fear. Come to New York. I'll show you the town, and you can make me laugh like you always do. Say yes."

She didn't look at him. She busied herself adjusting her T-shirt, but even the smooth touch of her own hands was too much a violation.

"You've no reason to say no," he maddeningly pointed out. "Say yes."

She faced him, praying for the same detachment on her own features. "Yes," she said.

"Wonderful." He smiled. Taking her hand once more in a formal embrace, he shook it. "Good night, then, partner."

He watched her walk toward the doorway, the polite smile still posed on his face, his body unmoving in its careful position. He waited until he heard the signaling creak of the stairs beneath her step. He waited even a minute more after that, keeping his breath regular, his muscles still. Finally all was silent.

He rose and walked quickly to the sideboard and its neat row of civilized crystal decanters. He grabbed one, ripped off its heavy-as-a-doorknob stopper, lifted the faceted bottle to his lips and drank deeply.

Chapter Eight

LEO & CLEO—Colin "all work, no play" Tremont, heir apparent to Leonard's of New York retailing empire, was seen sharing a cozy table at Nell's last night with a black-haired, kohl-eyed beauty not to be missed in electric blue, canary-yellow and thigh-high alligator-skin boots. Sources say the exotic lovely comes from Newport, which explains her attraction to old money and stiff upper lips. Don't break this columnist's heart and tell me next we'll see Shawn Tremont, Colin's bon vivant brother, in the boardroom?

A buzzer interrupted Colin's reading. He pushed down the intercom button. "Yes?"

"Ms. Rose has finished her tour of the store," his secretary informed him.

"Send her in."

The brass-inlaid door opened slowly as if about to give up a secret. Colin couldn't deny he was anticipating Aimee's beginning-of-the-day visit to his office. He attributed it to his curiosity about what costume, what new creature she would create. Escorted by his secretary, she came into the room. In leopard tuxedo pants, a black leather motorcycle jacket and a blond frenzy of hair replacing the black, Egyptian-style wig she'd worn last night, she didn't disappoint him. She smiled bold red lips at him. His day began.

Her gaze was on him, then past him, taken by the view beyond. She walked over to the massive window behind his desk to the famed skyline. When she turned back, he saw she was still smiling. He gestured toward a seat. She walked to the offered chair, her body fluid with life, full with texture and pattern, shaming the revered lines of Chippendale and Duncan Phyfe that kept court in this room.

Even he felt pompous and affected as he sat back down behind the English Regency desk that had been Hugo's and was to have been his father's. He stood up, walked to the front of the desk and leaned against its elegant edge. He bent one leg and angled it across the other; his arms folded across his chest. He'd gone from pompous to posed. Aimee, in leather and leopard, looked up and smiled, and he, with his corner office and commanding view and personal conference room with a complete, matching set of Chippendale chairs, was reminded he was no more than a man.

"You made the 'Dish of the Day' column," he told her, reaching behind him for the morning edition on the desk.

"My tastelessness knows no bounds," she said, taking the paper he handed her.

She read the item. When she looked up, her eyes had a wicked gleam. "This columnist—" she

glanced at the byline ""—Della Stevens... Maybe I
should invite her to tea in the Palm Court? Do you
think she'd come?"

"With bells on...except you'd probably already be
wearing them."

"You overestimate me."

"Not for one minute." Beneath the banter, there
was a note of seriousness.

Aimee laughed a lovely, musical sound. "Perhaps
in Newport they're ready to tar and feather me, but
here I'm borderline boring."

Colin shook his head. "You're far from boring."
Again the serious undercurrent was heard.

"Let me just say, I've picked up a few tricks on
this trip."

"Tricks I'm sure you'll share with Vivian when
we return to Newport?"

The playful light remained in Aimee's eyes. "Just
when she thought it was safe to step out in high
society again."

They both chuckled. Then, gazing at each other,
the laughter faded, and the room turned silent.

Colin took the paper from her hands and retreated
to behind the desk. He folded the paper into a neat
square. "So your room at the Plaza is satisfactory?"

"Satisfactory?" She mocked his suddenly formal
stance. "I'm too awed to even wear the complimen-
tary robe."

He permitted himself a small smile. "And you saw
the store?"

"I saw the store," she replied, again mimicking
his tone.

He nodded once. "Good." He looked down at several letters waiting for his signature on the desk.

"It's beautiful, Colin."

He looked up. "Yes, it is," he said, the detachment leaving his voice.

"And so big."

"Two hundred and thirty thousand square feet." The pride was ingrained in his voice.

"Well, I love every square inch of it," she told him.

"Thank you," he said, attempting a polite pronouncement even as, inside him, ridiculous gratitude welled up.

Of course she'd love the store. What starry-eyed shop clerk with dreams of being a designer wouldn't? He had never doubted her reaction. What surprised and annoyed him was his unfounded pleasure at her approval.

He knew she would also love the fashion houses she'd be touring tomorrow and the garment district with its come-hither racks of clothing waiting shamelessly in the street. She would love discussing fabric, hemlines, sleeve length with the reps and the buyers and listening to their deferential responses. She would love the mock-up of her own designs being created even as she sat before him with her sincere smile. He had promised her—and himself—physical restraint. Still, seduction was underway.

His secretary buzzed him once. "Representatives from the designer houses are with our buyers in the eighth-floor conference room."

"Thank you. Ms. Rose will be right there."

He rounded the desk once more. Aimee stood up.

"I've invited over people from the biggest and best fashion houses in New York. My buyers are briefing them now," he told her as he walked her to the door. "The reps will have designs and make suggestions, but you choose what you want." He opened the door that led to the reception area. "This is your show."

He watched his secretary lead Aimee away, then went back into his office. He had a meeting with the department managers in a few minutes and needed to sit down and review the reports to be discussed. Instead, he went to the wide window behind his desk.

Since Aimee and he had arrived in the city, he'd kept his word—he'd been the perfect gentleman, the polite escort, consoling himself that attraction could be accomplished with different means. But even that solace was not strong enough. His body felt bound, shackled by the effort of denying something inside of him so elemental, so right, he was awed by the sheer perfection of the emotion. Awed and terror-stricken.

He pressed his palms to the clear, cool glass like a man trying to break free. Unlike his current nemesis, he didn't have the luxury of outrageous costumes or masks of heavy makeup. Still, he was also the pretender.

SEVERAL NIGHTS LATER he led Aimee through the wide center aisle of the store. "I have something to show you," he told her.

It was their final evening together in New York. The time, like the relentless city itself, had pressed on at an accelerated pace. Even Aimee's dreams of the past few nights had adopted a feverish pitch, and she'd awakened within the extravagant width of the hotel bed, dazed and disorientated. She would dress swiftly and drink dark, strong coffee. But when she stepped out onto the street into the assault of people, cars, noise, color, it was as if the dream hadn't ended.

Once begun, the day would continue in the pattern formed despite the short time Aimee had been in New York: she spent the mornings and afternoons being squired about the city by one of the store's employees, enthusiastic, fast-talking girls or smooth-moving men, always stylishly attired. In between seeing the expected sights, there were meetings, discussions, plans formed for the fashion show. Occasionally she would get a glimpse of Colin. Sometimes they managed a quick chat, but usually he was far too busy for anything but an acknowledging smile.

But in the evening, when the city softened into a sea of lights, and the store would close, Colin and she would meet. Always for dinner, sometimes a show, but usually they just sat, lingering over a famous restaurant's renowned dessert. Lulled by a full stomach and warmed by wine, they would talk, telling each other about their day, the comings and goings, the small things of no particular consequence but needing to be shared.

The store was closed now. The lighting had been reduced to soft glows beneath the glass counters and a spotlight here and there. A security guard kept watch through electronic surveillance. Mannequins eyed Aimee and Colin with unblinking amusement.

He led her up the unmoving escalators, their footsteps echoing, until they reached the fourth floor. Here, the most popular designers had their own sections to display their latest creations.

Aimee moved past the Klein, Karan and Lauren outfits, nodding in appreciation as she passed each section.

But it was the movement of a circular platform spotlighted in the center of the room that called her attention. Three headless mannequins, twisted into various poses, silently revolved, proudly displaying their dresses. Each held in its lifeless hand, a single rose.

"Colin!" She clutched the tailored sleeve of his jacket. "Those are my designs."

She rushed forward, leaving him behind. She stood before the display, her hand lifting as if she had to touch the cloth to make certain it was real.

Colin came up beside her. "I hope you don't mind. I had these made up from some of the sketches you gave Vivian. They're only samples, and the fabric and details may not be your first choice—"

She hushed him. "They're beautiful."

She walked around the slow-moving circle, her eyes taking in each angle. She stepped back, seeing her clothes center stage among those of the world's most successful designers.

"They'll look even better," Colin noted, "on live models."

Aimee looked at him.

"Vivian's fashion show," he reminded her.

"Yes, but it still doesn't seem real." She reached out and allowed herself to touch a skirt hem. "This doesn't seem real."

"Your designs are good, Aimee."

She turned her face to him. "You really think so?" she asked as she had before.

He nodded. "What you lack in technical expertise can always be learned. You have a vitality and vision in your designs that can't be learned, only envied. It's the mark of a true original."

He moved away from her searching look. "If these fabrics, buttons, anything, don't please you, they can—"

"They please me," she answered, her gaze still on him.

"Good. We'll include them with the outfits being sent for the show. You must have others?"

She let out a quick laugh that said yes. "This is enough for now though." She looked at the clothing, then at Colin. "More than enough. Thank you. It's the kindest thing anyone has ever done for me."

She went to him and kissed the shadow of his cheek, resting her hand against the rough square of his jacket, feeling the quick beat of his heart through the expensive cloth.

His hands came up, encircled the bare slenderness of her upper arms. He gave her a long look, unreadable.

"You're a good man," she told him.

His fingers pressed into her flesh. She looked up into the night of his eyes. "If things were different...if circumstances hadn't been—"

He pushed her away, back until her hand left his heart. His hands still held her fast. His body stood immobile. The lines of his face deepened, casting his features with hard edges. The mannequins endlessly circled.

"It's too late for regrets."

His hands freed her. He turned and walked toward the escalator stairs. "We're returning to Newport tomorrow. We'll both need a good night's rest."

THEY LEFT at nine the next morning. By ten they'd left behind the heavy traffic and joined the interstate's open flow. The city only echoed in Aimee's head. Except for an occasional comment or benign observation, the car was silent. It wasn't a companionable, comfortable silence. It was the silence chosen when thoughts were confused and words were treacherous.

Aimee glanced at the man beside her. The soothing of sleep, the spill of new sun through the car hadn't served to alter his expression. Grimness wreathed his mouth. His gaze didn't veer from the road before them.

She had ruined everything last night with her wish for something that couldn't be. Until then, their time together had been perfect. He had promised her he'd be a host, an ambassador. He had broken his vow only to become a friend.

Then she, who had cautioned against false hope, had wished for more. Certainly the sight of her own designs temporarily nestled between the industry's top couturiers had swayed her, and she'd been right to express gratitude to Colin for his considerate efforts.

But she should've stopped there. She'd had no right to remind him of the futility of his freely confessed feelings. It was an attraction that must be denied—even as desire filled her.

Yet, in her heart, when she'd said those words, her wish had been real. If only she could separate Colin's feelings from his pressing need for a wife and child. If only the relationship had not so many motives.

If only...if only... She mocked herself. Her hopes were as tiresome today as they'd been last night.

The thought of being back in Newport washed over her. It wouldn't be much longer until this pantomime would end and she'd return to her old life. She waited for the bray of the gulls to laugh at her vain musings.

Finally she stretched her neck and saw the rocks and boulders still wet from high tide, the scrubby brush waiting to catch at bare legs, the dark footsteps leading to the beach's calmer water. She rolled down her window and breathed deeply. There was the tang of salt and sea, the low, forever roll of the waves. She half closed her eyes, nodding her head to the remembered rhythm.

When the car drove up to the estate, she saw several figures standing outside the house, their hands to their foreheads, shading the sun as they stared at the house's mammoth facade. Colin steered the car toward the garages in back only to find the path blocked by a large van. He pulled over to the side of the drive and parked.

"Looks like *Lifestyle* has arrived," he noted, watching as two men carried in a bag of long loaves of French bread, two bronze-trimmed urns and an azalea bush in full bloom.

"What're they doing?" Aimee asked, watching the men parade back and forth across the veranda.

"Accessorizing," Colin answered. "Remember, appearances are everything."

From between the opened French doors, Vivian appeared. Her gaze went past the van to Colin's car sitting in the drive. Her hand lifted, touching the triple strand of pearls at the base of her neck. Beside her, another woman appeared, shorter with a dark sleek cap of hair bobbed to her angular chin. She stepped briskly past Vivian and spoke to the two men, her chin thrusting out.

Colin looked at Aimee and winked, releasing some of the tenseness from his features. "Welcome home."

She smiled and opened the car door. With mincing steps, she started across the smooth-napped lawn leading to the house. Vivian watched her, her fingers twisting her pearl choker tight. Halfway there, Aimee stopped and flung her arms out wide. "Viv!" she cried. Her whole body dipped in a shimmy of excitement.

The other woman stopped her instructions to the two men and pointed her chin toward the high-pitched hello. The two men, at opposite ends of a long, tightly rolled bundle, also stopped.

The woman reached for the glasses strung about her neck by a gold chain and, lifting them to her thin nose, peered at Aimee. Aimee held her arms spread-eagled a few seconds longer for this black-bobbed woman to appreciate the full effect of her faux-furred, hot-panted, lamé tube-topped image.

Then, pushing her rhinestone, cat's-eye sunglasses

to the top of her blond beehive, Aimee allowed her body to wriggle once more as if it was shuddering excitement itself.

"I'm back," she cried out. The gulls shrieked above.

She resumed her small-stepped prance. Vivian stood motionless on the veranda except for the necklace winding tighter against her long, pale throat. The men, at each end of the coiled oblong, were set back into motion with an impatient motion of the dark-haired woman's hand.

"How do you do?" Aimee extended her hand as she flounced up the marble steps.

The small woman looked back at her hostess, but Vivian had closed her eyes, her lips pinched together in a pained expression.

The woman pushed her glasses to the tip of her nose and looked at Aimee over the top rims. "How do you do?" she questioned. Her hand came up, hesitated.

Aimee clutched that small, tense hand in both of hers and pumped it. "You aren't movie people, are you?"

"No." The woman tried to extract her hand from Aimee's grip, but Aimee held fast. "Vivian?" the woman called, her hair moving in a single, smooth sheaf as she turned her head.

Vivian came to life, moving forward with an all-occasion smile. "We didn't expect you back until the weekend, Aimee." Her voice strained as she forced Aimee's hands apart to release the woman. She turned to her guest, her smile still hovering.

"Please excuse Aimee. As you've witnessed, she's recently adopted a melodramatic approach to life."

"So you *are* from Hollywood!" Aimee exclaimed, grabbing the woman's hand once more and shaking it enthusiastically.

The woman jerked her hand away and took several steps back. Her glasses fell off the sharp tip of her nose and bounced against her flat, buttoned-up bosom.

"Aimee, this is Margo Wells with *Lifestyle* magazine."

"The press? You're the press?" Aimee stepped toward the woman who took another two steps back. "I love the press. I just got back from the Big Apple, and I met a whole bunch of lovely press people up there."

"You did?" Vivian questioned.

Aimee pulled up the top edge of her tube top and released it with a snap. Then, cupping her hands beneath her bosom, she adjusted her breasts. "Tube tops." She winked at the two staring women. "My second favorite invention after the home bikini wax kit."

"Who'd you meet in New York?" Vivian's smile was so tight, she talked through her teeth.

"Let's see." Aimee pulled her sunglasses from the tower of her hair and tapped them against her temple. "I had tea yesterday with Della Stevens at the Plaza. Can you imagine me…at the Plaza?" She did a little curtsy.

Margo smiled without sweetness. "The image has a Dali-esque flavor."

"Dolly? Oh, she's my favorite country singer, too!

With those fabulous blond hairdos and that set of big—''

''Who else did you meet there?'' Vivian interrupted desperately.

''So many people.'' Aimee made a wide curve with her sunglasses.

''What other members of the 'press'?'' Vivian said the word as if she'd just tasted something sour.

''Well, I called Cecilia Rathmore to thank her for the little item she had on me and the boys last week—''

''Thank her?'' Vivian's modulated voice abruptly soared.

Aimee unconcernedly studied herself in the reflection of her sunglasses. ''But she wasn't in town.''

''Thank goodness,'' Vivian breathed.

''So I left her a message to stop in the next time she's in our little corner of the world.''

''You did what?'' Vivian distinctly pronounced each word.

Aimee folded close her sunglasses and hooked them into the top of her tube top. ''Wouldn't it be great if she made it for the fashion show? I told her and the others all about it.''

''The others?'' The skin around Vivian's mouth and nose whitened.

''Della Stevens, of course. And then there were some nice people who called from *Hot Stuff* and *Do Tell.*''

What sounded like a snort came from Margo.

Vivian moved to the veranda railing and held on.

''I didn't have time to meet with all of them personally, but we did talk on the phone.''

Vivian turned to Aimee, the circle of white revealed around her eyes giving her a wild look. "There are no people at *Hot Stuff* and *Do Tell*. Only piranhas." Her chest pulsed beneath her cashmere shell as she took inaudible, shallow breaths.

"Margo." She turned to her guest. "Would you please excuse me for a minute?" She smiled as she wrapped her hand around Aimee's wrist and pulled her toward the open French doors.

Her low pumps tapping, she led Aimee through the kitchen, past the curious stares of the servants and into a vaulted room. Leaving her in the center of a dim patterned carpet, Vivian closed the tall door to the room.

She turned around, getting Aimee squarely in her sight. "You're through," she pronounced in a low, cutting tone.

"I'm only beginning," Aimee disagreed.

"You're not the person I thought you were." Vivian walked toward her.

"No, I'm not." Aimee turned as Vivian circled her.

"I offered you everything," the older woman said.

"Did you?"

"Money, status, power."

"Vivian, Vivian," Aimee muttered in disappointed tones. "What am I going to do with you?"

"I offered you more than anyone else will ever be able to give you."

Aimee kept turning as Vivian circled faster. "If I believed that, Vivian, I'd pack it all in—metallic mini and black motorcycle jacket included."

Vivian stopped circling. "You have a black motorcycle jacket?"

Aimee started to laugh. "Oh, Vivian, you and I might become friends yet."

Vivian looked down the high arch of her nose. "Pack up all your...*things*." She pronounced the word with pure distaste. "I've been patient, attributing your antics to the high-spiritedness of youth—"

"Plus you don't want to lose a billion-dollar fortune," Aimee noted.

"No, I don't. I hope that doesn't shock you."

Aimee had to laugh again. "Vivian, I'll say it again—one day, you and I are going to be great buddies."

"But I also will not risk losing my reputation. I'll not stand for any further scandal in this house. My offer has been retracted, but as a goodwill gesture, I will give you one hundred thousand dollars."

"Vivian." Aimee threw her hands up in defeat. "I was almost starting to like you, too."

"It's a more than generous offer, and it'll allow you to begin that little bistro you mentioned."

"Boutique," Aimee corrected.

"Whatever." Vivian made a dismissing motion with her long, narrow hand. "It's better than nothing."

"Is it?" Aimee questioned.

"So..." Vivian started toward the door. "We're agreed."

"Not so fast, Viv. I don't see any lily-white flags waving from this side of the room."

The older woman turned around. "You're going to be tiresome, aren't you?"

"No, just threatening. I still have the contract, re-member, and now I have several friends waiting with bated breath for any anecdotes about the Tremont dynasty."

"What contract?"

"Now, Vivian, you're being tiresome."

"Call my lawyers. Have your new *friends* call my lawyers. Have them talk to every person employed at the firm. Not one of them will know anything about any contract." Vivian folded her arms across cashmere and genuinely smiled. "Get your bags out of Colin's car, but don't bother unpacking."

She turned, and with a properly paced step, left Aimee standing in the center of the faded carpet.

The door closed. Failure welled within Aimee like an unvoiced sob. She had lost. Money and power had won once more. She had thought she could make a difference, a stand, show those with the money and the power they must wield it wisely.

But at the final curtain, it was she who'd learned the lesson.

She gathered her disillusioned ideals and walked to the veranda. Head high, she would gather her bags, say goodbye to Hugo, Shawn, James, Colin… Colin…now her heart wept anew, now that the threat was over, no longer needing to deny desire. She loved him. She knew that, had always known that, and with a newborn stoicism, accepted it.

For she also knew Colin needed a wife and child. She hadn't thought him capable of a marriage of con-venience, but in the past few days, she'd learned that the store, the employees, all his work was as central to him as his soul. He wouldn't give them up easily. And so, all his professions of attraction...they were suspect.

Vivian was right. It was over. She would go home now.

She heard the murmur of voices and not-too-loud laughter as she approached the veranda. Vivian and Margo were still on the back porch. She thought about turning back, but then changed her mind. She hadn't won, no, but she wasn't the one who should be ashamed.

She'd reached the open French doors when she heard Colin's low tenor, and, as she stepped through the opening, she saw he had joined the two women. She hesitated, but the car was still parked on the side of the drive. She wanted to get her bags out of it before it went to the garage. She wanted to be gone. She started across the wide expanse.

"Now you've met Hugo and Colin." Vivian was counting on her fingers. "And my son, Shawn, will be here after the regatta."

Aimee attempted to pass the trio, but Colin reached out. His arm wrapped around her, pulling her close to his side. She could feel her face and chest fill with heat, and she looked up at him questioningly, but he was looking at the *Lifestyle* editor.

"And you've met the newest member of the Tremont family tree."

A thick, strangled sound rose from Vivian's throat. "Colin, please, it takes more than fishnet stockings and a temporary position as my assistant to lay claim to the Tremont family crest."

"You didn't tell them, did you?" Colin looked down at Aimee, a toothy grin on his face. "The way my little minx was dancing around this porch, I was certain she'd spilled the beans." He touched the tip of Aimee's nose with his finger, kissed her forehead.

Vivian cleared her throat again. "What beans, Colin?" Her features tightened, and the long bones in her face, once more, became prominent.

Colin smiled at his stepmother. "Aimee and I are engaged."

Chapter Nine

She might have dreamed it: the man, handsome, compelling, his arm around her, holding her as if she were the dream about to steal away. Then, there were the words *Aimee and I are engaged.*

But he was saying them again, with the smile of a man who's captivated and doesn't even care. With love's grin, he was telling Vivian and Margo about the trip to New York. He told them of intimate dinners, long, lovely talks, late-night walks when the city took a breath. Even Aimee began to believe him.

At the first announcement of the engagement, Vivian's body had drawn itself up, her bones becoming an elegant brace. As Colin continued to talk, Aimee watched Vivian's body calcify. Her legs locked at the knees. Her arms bent into rigid right angles. Her features were inflexible; her complexion thin-veined as the marble rail she reached for and grasped again.

"My, my, a wedding," Margo remarked, cautious in her comments. "Congratulations." She pushed her heavy sheaf of hair behind her ear and glanced at Vivian.

Aimee stood sheltered beneath Colin's arm, no

longer standing alone against the menace barely below Vivian's constructed expression. The seething beneath her still bosom was imperceptible and all the more effective. It wouldn't be shown, not here, not yet, but Aimee knew fury imploded within the woman—an icy cold fury.

Colin, as if sensing Aimee's fear and confusion, leaned over her, hiding her from the two other woman.

"Don't worry," he said as his arms wrapped around her and pantomimed an embrace. "I'm here to help you."

Aimee looked up into his face. The darkness of his eyes was too close.

He brought the night closer, leaning down until it seemed their mouths had to meet in a kiss. Instead, in the breath of space between them, he whispered, "I've always been here to help you."

Her lips had to reach for him, but his mouth moved away. It brushed her cheek, her ear, tightening the slow coil of desire within her until her hand lifted and took the white cotton of his shirt in a fist.

He whispered in her ear, "Did you see Vivian's face? She looked like they'd threatened to take Gucci off the market."

He made her laugh. Then his mouth came down on her open, laughing mouth.

When they separated, Aimee realized, if this was a dream, it was a very dangerous dream.

Margo was discretely checking a leather-covered notebook she'd pulled from her bag. Vivian still stared at the couple.

"This is a good story," Margo decided, tapping a

slim, gold pen against the edge of the notebook. She didn't bother to look at Vivian this time. She pointed the pen at Aimee. "You were Vivian's assistant?"

Aimee nodded.

"It's got color, it's got human interest, and even our readers go for that Cinderella shtick." She wrote something in her notebook, then looked back up at Aimee and Colin.

"We'll cover the wedding. Of course you'll give us an exclusive on the engagement announcement?"

The woman gave up her urbane smile for a broad grin. Aimee saw her teeth wonderfully white, contrasting with the black gloss of her hair. Her back teeth were chisel sharp.

Colin looked down at Aimee still within the heavy circle of his arm. "You'll have to speak with my bride-to-be about such matters. I'm leaving all the wedding details up to her discretion."

"Discretion?" Vivian repeated, the only word she'd said since the announcement. Her hand had lifted, lay flat against the pearls cool and polished around her neck.

"Have you set a date? Picked a dress? Decided where to have the ceremony? Who's catering?" Margo's pen was poised over her opened notebook.

"It's all been so sudden. Nothing's been decided," Aimee answered.

"We could do a series of articles," Margo said, inspired. "We were right here at the beginning. We could start with the engagement announcement, then chronicle your progress to the big day. The ups, downs, ins, outs—it'll be a classic example of marriage among the moneyed. Say yes, and I'll call New York right now and pitch it to the senior editor.''

Aimee looked from Margo to Vivian. She felt Colin beside her, strong, solid, not a dream. A real person with motives—perhaps dangerous, perhaps no more benign than her own. After all, he hadn't asked her for anything, but only offered the cool relief of friendship, the support of a secret accomplice. He hadn't assumed anything, expected anything. Had she been guilty of the same wrong she was trying to right? Had she reversed the prejudice? Had she misjudged the man?

All she knew was it felt more than wonderful, more than right to stand close beside him now, facing Vivian.

''Everything's happened so quickly.'' She again addressed Margo. ''And there are my new friends in New York to consider—Della, Cecilia...''

Aimee felt Colin's arm slide away. He knew she could stand on her own now.

''Hacks,'' Margo pronounced. ''Let *Lifestyle* give this story the royal treatment it deserves.''

''Well...'' Aimee's shoulders moved in a restrained roll of excitement. ''I do have some ideas I'm dying to share with someone.''

''While they're setting up for the interior photo shoot,'' Margo suggested, ''why don't you and I have a little chat?''

Aimee looked at Vivian. ''Why not?''

One of Vivian's slender fingers was wrapped in a circle of pearls. The finger coiled the beads around its length, twisting the pearls tighter and tighter.

''You wouldn't happen to know,'' Aimee asked

Margo as they walked toward the French doors, "if they still make those delightful glow-in-the-dark silk roses?"

On the porch, there was a sound like soft rain. Aimee stopped and turning, saw Vivian stone still while the pearls, broken free, scattered and bounced about her feet.

"TWO MILLION DOLLARS."

Aimee hadn't heard Vivian's Belgium-leathered steps, but she knew she'd come. She turned around and found her in the bedroom doorway, imperial, unsmiling.

"Two million dollars."

Aimee lifted a pile of nylon, six-for-two-dollars, bikini underwear from the dresser drawer and placed them in the duffel on the bed. She went back to the bureau, pulled out a colorful tangle of hose and carried them to the bag.

"Did you hear me?" Vivian took three steps into the room.

Aimee glanced up. "You told me to leave, Vivian."

She continued to pack, her movements economical and measured, belying her anger. Her steps were as steady as her resurrected resolve.

She wasn't really leaving…just as she wasn't really marrying Colin. Only, Vivian didn't know that.

Now she'd come to coax her to stay.

"I'm doubling the offer."

"I don't need your money."

"That's right, you don't, do you? Now that you're

going to be Mrs. Colin Tremont.'' Sarcasm glazed Vivian's words.

Aimee went to the closet and began removing clothes. "It was your idea."

"It was my idea, wasn't it?"

Aimee was bent over, looking in the corner of the closet for a stray sandal, but she heard the leading tone in the other woman's words.

"Actually, it's all rather amusing," Vivian said in a garden-party voice. "I wonder if Colin would be amused by the situation." She paused, as if contemplating the idea.

"And there's the contract, of course. Why, he'd probably find that a howl. What do you think, Aimee dear?"

Aimee looked up from her packing, and repeated the words said to her by Vivian only hours ago. "What contract?"

Vivian looked at her opponent. "Touché."

"No, match point," Aimee said.

Vivian smiled, but her features stayed sharp. "And the ball's in your court, isn't it?"

Aimee concentrated on removing a pair of pants from a hanger.

"Two million dollars," Vivian offered. "It's all I've got."

Aimee looked up at the older woman. "No, it's not."

Vivian studied her. "There's something else you want, isn't there?" Her eyes narrowed, the pupils contracting. Her hands folded prayer-like, her chin resting on the tips of her fingers. "What do you want?" she wondered.

Her hands separated. One finger pointed at Aimee. "The bistro," she said, a tiny, triumphant curl to her lips.

Even in her angered state, Aimee had to smile.

"With two million dollars, you can open bistros up and down the coast," Vivian told her.

"Boutique," Aimee corrected. "I want a small boutique to sell my designs."

She looked at one of her dresses hanging in the closet. She remembered its sister gracefully circling in the center of Leonard's designer collections. When she'd seen her creations displayed in one of the world's foremost clothing stores, it'd made her realize how much she wanted this dream. At the same time it'd made her realize the disparity between the dream and reality. Her designs had been removed before the store opened its doors the next morning. It was the Klein, Karan, Lauren designs that had remained. With nothing more than a young girl's dream, Aimee Rose's clothes would stay in the darkness of the closet.

She turned away from the dress and went back to the bureau. She closed the top drawer and opened the second. "I know this is a foreign concept to you, Viv, but money isn't everything." From the drawer, she shook out a pair of zebra-striped leggings. She held the pants up against her own legs. "I don't think I had a chance to show you these yet." She pointed her toe and kicked one leg out. "I searched all over SoHo for a bustier to match."

Vivian watched her. "So you intend to marry Colin?"

Aimee looked up at that bony, bloodless face.

"He's been so sweet to me," she taunted. "Do you know, in New York, he even had three of my designs sewn up and displayed in Leonard's on our last night there? Is that a guy or what?"

Vivian angled her long, oval face. Her lips pulled up, drawing tiny rays of age about them. "I can give you something Colin can't."

Aimee folded the leggings and put them into her bag. "Now you're scaring me, Viv."

"I can wear your designs."

Aimee's hands, hidden within the bag, stopped. Not trusting her expression, she kept her head bowed, her gaze focused on the folded clothes. Beneath them lay her sketchbook. She always packed it first.

"No, that's one thing Colin can't do," she agreed, her head still bent, her voice deliberately amused. "Except for certain clubs in the Village."

"I'll wear your outfits to the premier social events. They'll be photographed from all angles, oohed and aahed at. The designer will be declared the latest sensation. All summer season, your name will be listed with fashion's most famed. By fall, a Rose could be ranked right up there with Dior, Chanel, Gucci."

"I can see it in neon now. Everything's Coming Up Roses." Aimee maintained her carefree composure. Inside the bag, her hands were shaking.

"The fashion show will introduce your designs," Vivian continued. "I'm sure you've scads more sketches than those few you showed me."

Aimee was finally able to look up. Vivian's expression was patrician and pleased.

"I can make you," the older woman said.

Aimee knew what the woman said was true. She'd

known it since the first time she'd sat across from Vivian, her folder of sketches balanced on trembling knees.

She also knew if she wanted to succeed with her plan, she'd have to agree to this new offer. To reject without a valid reason would raise suspicion.

What worried Aimee was that she didn't want to reject it. She wanted to see her creations come to life as much as she wanted to reach the goal of her plan.

She had as little intentions of marrying Shawn as she had Colin. But would it be so wrong if, in the meantime, she designed beautiful clothes for Vivian? When Aimee didn't marry Shawn, Vivian would withdraw her support, but until then...

She rummaged to the bottom of her bag for her sketch pad. She pulled it out and flipped over its cover. "These are rough, but with a little refinement and the right material, you'd look like a million...you'd look great."

Vivian took the pad from Aimee's hands and flipping the pages, scanned the pictures. When finished, she gave the book back. "Are we agreed then?"

Her eyes, the color of rain, watched Aimee. "We'll continue with the terms of the original agreement, plus the matter we just discussed here." She extended a long-fingered hand.

Holding the pad in one hand, Aimee's other hand moved toward Vivian's palm. It was necessary if she was going to accomplish her intended end, she told herself. Nobody would get hurt. Their hands met, and Aimee learned the touch of temptation was cool and creamy smooth.

Later that day, she made her way down the steep,

stony footpath to the sea and sat, sketchbook on her lap. She drew in the day's paling light and dreamed of old women made young, raw women made smooth, common men made dashing, all from no more than the drape and cut and color of cloth. The misgivings that'd prickled her neck hairs earlier were no more than the white dot of a sail far out on the water's surface.

She had been there almost an hour, away from the house—too big, yet without any place to hide—when she heard the soft shift of stones and turned to see Colin coming down the bluff to her. He had to have been looking for her if he found her here, half-hidden by a large boulder cast pink by the day's leaving light. He raised his hand in greeting and gave a quick smile, but even before that, at the first sight of his figure, feeling had welled and rolled through Aimee like the high-tide waves.

"Here you are," he said, dropping down beside her onto the pebbly sand. He propped his arms on his pulled-up knees. His hands hung relaxed. He wore pants of a light weave, rolled at the ankles, and a gray V-necked sweater. He never sunned, but his skin was naturally tanned as if the sun couldn't bear to see him pale. He looked at her and smiled again. Aimee felt her heart stumble and fall, and she wondered, not for the first time, how she would ever leave this man when the time came.

"There was a phone call for you at the house." His smile turned teasing. "Some deep-voiced man."

"Did you tell him I'm an engaged woman?"

"Are you?" He continued to play.

"That's what Margo Wells is going to tell the many readers of *Lifestyle*."

"If it's in print, it must be true," Colin noted. "I didn't think Vivian was going to survive the surprise, but I'm sure she's recovered by now."

"She wasn't the only one surprised."

He looked at her. "It was what we'd discussed before leaving for New York. We'd talked about getting you back early to get national coverage for the engagement announcement from the *Lifestyle* people. I'm sorry if—"

"Don't apologize," she said. "I should be thanking you. Your timing couldn't have been more perfect. Just prior to your little bombshell, Vivian had told me to pack up and head 'em out."

"She had?" He let out a low chuckle. "Why?"

"It was either the tube top or the beehive. But don't worry, she bounced back to her old self and rallied with a two-million-dollar offer for me to forgive and forget."

Colin looked out to the sea. "Another million dollars. I guess you did have a good day."

"Double or nothing. Only, I told her to save her money."

"You did?" His face turned toward her once again.

"I told her the original million would be enough for my modest needs."

Colin looked out to the water. "Of course."

"So she offered me something else."

He turned back to her, but this time she was staring out at the horizon.

"She's willing to wear my designs. And the fashion show, as you'd said, will be used to introduce me personally and professionally.''

Colin nodded. ''Very clever.''

She heard the hard, cutting *c* in his response. She looked at him. ''Who? Her or me?''

His smile was slow, softening any hard sounds in his speech. ''Both of you.''

Aimee shivered, knowing she should've worn a heavier sweater. The night temperatures were coming quickly. The white caps of the water rose.

''I wasn't sure... I'm still not sure if it was the right thing to accept her offer, but I couldn't think of a believable reason to refuse. Then I thought, would it be anything more than you displaying my designs for my pleasure? It's not like I'm going to put the woman in polyester pants and see-through blouses.''

Colin gave her a crestfallen look, making her smile.

''Now we both know Vivian's got enough to hide in her closet already,'' she scolded him. ''I'll dress her in my best—not that it matters. Once I fail to marry her son, those clothes, along with my career, will go down in flames.''

''You're worrying about taking advantage of someone else,'' Colin remarked, ''yet you might be the one to lose in the end.''

She shook her head. Her hair, wound in a careless topknot, a mechanical pencil stuck through its middle, fell about her face. ''I intend to win.''

''I'm just saying...''

He touched the top of her hand, a touch as light and quick as a dragonfly landing. Still, Aimee's desire rose like a wildness inside her. She feared it'd shown in her eyes because his hand drew back and he stopped his sentence. He turned his gaze mercifully back to the ocean. She looked that way, too, fighting her need and her want. She focused on the water darkening; the sharp smell of kelp in the cooler air.

"I assume you amused Ms. Wells all afternoon with your proposed plans for the wedding?" He changed the subject.

"She didn't think the original Village People would reunite to play our reception. I told her maybe I could live without the cowboy, but I had to have the construction worker and the Indian chief, or my special day would be ruined."

"So this is a retro wedding?"

Aimee assumed a thoughtful expression. "I always considered the Village People to have a timeless appeal...but I like the theme idea."

Colin was smiling as he watched the sea. "It has infinite possibilities."

They sat together for a few minutes, not speaking. The line of the water where it cut the horizon was silver. She heard Colin's even breaths beside her. She couldn't help but think if they were lovers, they'd be in each other's arms now. Colin touched her shoulder and she started.

"I'm sorry." He pulled back his hand again.

"No, it's me." She brushed aside his apology. "Nervous bride." The light laugh that followed her comment had a high-strung quality. She should go. It was too dangerous, sitting here alone as the darkness fell and the sea softly sang.

She closed her pad. "You said I had a phone call?"

"It was your brother, Jack."

She nodded. "I'd left a message on his machine earlier." Her fingers skittered over the sketchbook cover, brushing away grains of sand. "I should go up and give him a call."

Colin rubbed his forehead. "I should go in, too. I've got more meetings in the morning, the ground breaking ceremony in the afternoon, then I've got to get back to New York."

"You're leaving already?" Aimee didn't have time to check the disappointment in her voice.

He nodded, gratefully not acknowledging her dismay. "At the end of the week, I have to fly out to the West Coast."

"I see." But she had to ask, "When will you be back?"

"I'll only be spending a few days in L.A., and I'll probably make a stop in our Chicago outlet on the way back, so I'll be back in New York midweek."

"When will you be back in Newport?"

"I don't know." He was watching her now, his features, always arrogant, naturally impenetrable.

"It's just I was hoping you'd be here for the fashion show." Even she could hear nervous keen in her voice.

"Aimee." He cupped the curve of her cheek. Her eyes, avoiding him, now were forced to look at his face. "I wouldn't miss it for the world."

She smiled, her cheek becoming fuller in his palm.

"We're partners, remember?" He spoke to her softly, his words as rhythmic as the water.

"Then there's the wedding." She filled the closing space between them with words. "What if I have a question and have to speak to you about a date or a detail?"

"Call New York. My secretary will always know how to reach me."

"Of course," Aimee again agreed. She needed to stand up, move away, shake herself out of this schoolgirl's daze. She didn't move.

Neither did Colin. As if he knew, with no more than a slight stroke of her cheek, she'd be in his arms, curling tight against that wide-berthed chest, kissing that mouth now still.

She didn't know she was trembling until he said, "You're shivering."

"It's the cold," she lied. She stood up too swiftly. Her head whirled. She held out her hands. There was nothing but air. Slowly her sight cleared, the spinning subsided. She saw Colin standing before her, his hands outstretched as if to catch her if she fell. She moved back to the hard wall of the bluff.

"Are you all right?" he asked, coming to her, his eyes concerned.

"Yes," she lied again. The dizziness was gone, but the desire remained. "I should've worn a heavier sweater." She backed up, pressing herself into the bluff.

"Are you sure you're okay?" he asked again. He was so close now, only a swell of breath prevented their bodies from meeting. He brushed the strands of hair from her forehead. He smelled of summer wind.

She looked into his eyes, seeking the darkness, wanting oblivion from cautious thought. His head bowed down, the darkness coming closer, expanding. His lips were almost to hers when, with a last remnant of strength, she turned her head, pressing her cheek into cool stone.

"Please don't," she pleaded, not because she didn't want him to, but because she did.

He moved back. He said nothing. She looked at him, seeing from his face, the distance between them was far greater than a few separating steps.

"I'll walk you up to the house," he said.

She wanted to refuse his escort, but she saw the set of his features.

They didn't speak until they reached the house more in darkness than light. Even then, all Colin said was "Good night."

"You're not coming in?" Aimee was still at the opened door.

"No," he answered. He didn't offer anything more.

"Good night," she said, not hesitating for fear she'd turn to him, go to him, her lips moist, her eyes wet with apology.

He waited until the door shut after her, then turned and made his way back to the beach. His movements seemed jerky; his muscles felt like stretched wire. His blood thrummed in his veins. He wouldn't be able to sit, so he walked, seeking relief from the soft give of sand beneath his feet.

He removed his moccasins, unbuttoned his pants and let them fall loose. He pulled the sweater over his head and threw it on the sand with the rest of his clothes. Naked, he walked into the water.

The water swirled about his ankles with a cold

shock he welcomed. He walked until the waves were at his waist, then dove into the dark water and swam with long, steady strokes, fighting the sea's rhythm. He swam until his muscles ached, his arms and legs were weighted and his thoughts were no longer of the woman.

But he turned onto his back, letting the water carry him, and saw her face in the stars above. His body floated, numb, only his feelings threatening to drown him.

He'd come too close, was losing control. Passion had killed his father, and it would kill him, too, if he wasn't cautious. Unlike his father, he wasn't willing to give up everything for a few moments' pleasure.

But was that all it was? the rock of the waves seemed to ask him. Knowing the sea couldn't be lied to, he thought no. If it was nothing more than a few moments' pleasure, he'd have taken Aimee long ago, brought her into his bed and satisfied the witching need within him.

No, with this woman, it was more than momentary pleasure. It was something much more, surrounded by high stakes and too many things that weren't what they seemed. It was an enemy he wasn't certain how to fight.

Yet he would fight it, and he wouldn't lose. She'd told him earlier, "I intend to win."

But so did he.

Chapter Ten

The plane began its descent into Kennedy. Colin took one last look at the paper in his hand, then shoved it into the seat pouch before him. Still, Aimee smiled out at him. Shawn was beside her in the picture, his arm slung around her bared shoulders. The fruit-decorated sombrero she wore shadowed her eyes. Her smile was in the light.

It wasn't the first picture of Aimee he'd seen while he was away. There had been others, she always outrageously dressed and usually accompanied by Shawn. Then, yesterday, the new issue of *Lifestyle* had come out with Vivian on the cover, perched in an eighteenth-century chair with an insufferable expression on her face and a three-foot bluefish on her lap. The cover copy had read Holy Mackerel! Matrimony In The Bounty!

Aimee had risen to new heights while he was away.

He'd been away longer than planned, longer than necessary, purposefully putting time and miles between him and Aimee. Yet he had looked, and there'd been grainy black-and-whites of her on his desk, in the corner kiosks. Worse, there were the pictures of her in his mind, four-color, three-dimensional, maddening. And in them, he beside her, not his flaxen half brother with the smile supplied by well-aged Scotch and a false sense of security.

The plane landed, the breath of New York now dominating all senses. He gathered his luggage. Usually he'd head for the taxis lined up outside the terminal, but instead he went to the first car rental booth he saw. If he drove fast, he could be in Newport before dark.

AIMEE NODDED and smiled, but she had stopped listening to the man next to her several minutes ago. Her dinner partner was a great-nephew of a former vice president of the United States, a fact which seemed to define the man's whole existence. He continued his anecdote about a Congressional aide and an overflowing toilet in the White House.

She doubted the man would notice if she looked away. Still, she kept her glances around the table furtive as if she were kitchen help peeking through a crack in the door. Shawn was diagonally opposite her, his glass empty once again. Without being summoned, a tuxedoed servant stepped forward, filled it, then stepped back as if he'd never even been there. Shawn's eyes were red-veined, his only show of physical frailty. His smile rivaled the sun. He caught her look and gave her a wink. Her gaze went back to the great-nephew of the former vice president of the United States.

Only to shift away once more. Vivian presided at the far end of the table. She wore a dramatic design

Aimee had only finished sewing this morning. The
material, a black-and-gold brocatelle, had been spe-
cially ordered from New York. It was a heavy, elaborate fabric echoing the dignity of its wearer. The
gown was simple, its straight lines and high Man-
darin collar almost sexless except every time Vivian
moved, turned, breathed, black and gold swirled, taking more than its share of the light, and the dress
began to dance. The light then lifted, continued to
the sapphire-cut diamonds in Vivian's ears and
spread to her upswept hair, weaving fine gold threads
throughout it.

When shown the dress, Vivian had only granted it
a cursory nod, but in it her movements were more
animated, her smile not so bridled. It hadn't mollified
the paling wrath that had come when Vivian saw the
cover of *Lifestyle*. That had only been done by an
immediate call to *Lifestyle*'s new editor in chief, demanding an explanation. Unsatisfied with his defense
of a tongue-in-cheek slant to draw reader attention,
Vivian declared an abrupt end to the magazine's
journalistic freedom within the realm of Newport.
Aimee didn't doubt the brash, new editor in chief's
days were also limited.

Aimee's relationship with the press, however,
didn't reflect any such antipathy. On the contrary, her
easy access, vamping postures and outrageous costumes had made her a media darling. She also always
made sure to tip off the photographers and columnists before her frequent forays into Newport society,
more to guarantee Vivian's chagrin than her own
popularity.

Vivian, ever the master, publicly attributed

Aimee's antics to her "creative calling." This statement, appearing in interviews in *Femme Fashion* and *In the Closet,* and repeated often wherever Newport society gathered, earned tolerance for Aimee and sympathy for Vivian.

Vivian also used Aimee's social stepping out and Colin's absence as an excuse for Shawn to serve as an escort. Aimee knew Shawn's squiring her to numerous social functions had nothing to do with propriety. Vivian was simply setting the stage to explain Aimee's sudden elopement with Shawn on the morning of her intended marriage to Colin. Except for the cover of her cradling a fish, everything seemed to be going Vivian's way. A fact that made Aimee realize even more she had to follow her plan through to the end. For now, she was grateful she could focus on the fashion show and fortify her defenses in this seeming cease-fire.

Thinking all these thoughts, it took her a minute to realize the great-nephew of the former vice president of the United States was no longer talking. She looked to him to feign an answer to the question that had caused the pause, but his eyes were looking past her to the front of the room. As she followed his gaze, she noticed other conversations had stopped, laughter had halted. The music of knives and forks against etched china had softened. The candlelight slowed its flutter.

Aimee's gaze continued the length of the table. The only other movement she saw was the practiced lift of thin, arched brows. She followed the stares. There, centered in the open door, was the object that had caused the party's seamless symphony to miss a beat. Aimee's own heart gave pause. Colin had come home.

His clothes were wrinkled as if worn too long. His hair fell long across his brow, needing to be smoothed back off his forehead. Fine lines of fatigue pulled at his features, carving his mortal stature beneath the imperial hold of his head, the bold breath of his gaze. He was a man as much feared as admired. Aimee looked at him. With the sudden clarity that comes from separation and reunion, she also knew he was a man who'd never been loved. Until now.

He found her. She stood and was before him before she'd even realized she had risen. It was only when she was so close she could touch him that she hesitated. Then his arm reached out and pulled her to him, tight against his body, and his mouth was on hers. He kissed her deeply, fiercely, while the most genteel, most refined members of Newport's upper crust looked on, delicately clearing their throats.

Somewhere, far beyond the beating of blood in her temples, the moan in her breast, Aimee heard Vivian say, "They're engaged, you know."

The kiss went on and on, a breath itself. When it ended, Aimee bowed her forehead, depleted. She rested there against the erratic rise and fall of his chest. He stroked her hair, supporting her with an arm wrapped low around her waist.

She knew she must move. There was a dinner table of the curious and the cutting behind her; there was a man she couldn't love in front of her. Still her body stayed motionless, unwilling to separate from the flesh and muscle of the man who'd been gone too long. She rested on him now. Her legs were weak, her thoughts irrational.

When his arm slipped beneath her knees, and he lifted her and carried her out of the tastefully adorned dining room, she knew there would be talk about this for many Newport summers to come.

He carried her down the generous hall. Her head buried in his neck, not knowing what would happen next, not caring, only wanting the bronze of his skin against her mouth and the wrap of his arms around her.

She heard him say, "Hello, James."

She heard James respond with his customary calmness, "Hello, Master Colin. Nice to see you back."

Colin walked on, and Aimee thought with the passion of lunacy, *Don't put me down. Don't put me down.* For she knew, if her feet hit solid ground, reason would be restored. Reason with its whys this could never be.

Colin stopped, but she still couldn't bear to move her mouth away from the ribbed surface of his neck. She felt herself lowered until she was sitting on the hard bed of his thighs, and he was beneath her, supported by overstuffed chintz.

Still having thwarted solid ground, she allowed herself to look up. Her head was above his now. She laid a hand on either side of his face and tenderly kissed those lips until her heart stiffened with pain and pleasure.

She lifted her mouth from his. One thumb outlined his lips. "You certainly make a hell of an entrance," she whispered. "And your exit isn't too shabby, either."

"We're only behaving like any normal engaged couple."

"We're not any normal engaged couple." Her thumb stopped its caress.

"To all outward appearances, we are. We're excused certain behaviors."

"And to hell with them if they can't take a joke," she rallied, forcing any apprehension from her voice.

He touched her brow, traced her hairline. "Have you been hanging out on the docks while I've been away? Is that where the salty language and the fish Vivian is rocking to sleep on the cover of *Lifestyle* came from?"

Aimee laughed, her head rearing back, and the tears springing to her eyes, releasing both anguish and amusement. "It's a long story."

"But a good one I'll bet."

"Yes." She was sober now, staring at him. The giddiness of passion was also beginning to subside, but her emotions remained at the edge, threatening to topple her. She had to look away. She struggled to steady herself.

"Aimee?" he asked. He didn't embrace her further. His hands fell away from her body and rested on the flowered chair arms as if separate entities.

"Aimee?" he asked again, but she wouldn't look at him. She was afraid.

"I promised you control," she heard him say. "I gave you control. I've proved to be a friend and a partner."

He paused, then said, "I want more. I've always wanted more."

She saw two of his fingers lift and twitch.

"You want more also."

She didn't protest.

"I vowed control. I've strained that promise to the point where, if I go further, my word will be broken. I will not break my promise. If there's to be more between us, it is you who must break the bonds. It is you who must make the choice."

She heard his words. She sat, her profile to him, her heart contracting. She wanted nothing more than to close her eyes and fall down deep into the draw of her desire.

She forced her eyes to stay open. She saw a room where she didn't belong, would never belong. She saw a room where she'd been summoned to be bought and sold like common goods.

She turned her head, giving Colin more than her profile. She saw a man who needed a wife to secure his financial and professional status. She saw a man she could never have in the way her heart pleaded. Even as passion moved through her, pulling at her muscles as if they were marionette's strings, she knew too much had been before and too much was to come for her and Colin to ever have a chance. Their joy would never be untainted.

With the tears from her maniacal laughter still in her eyes, she said, "If we go back right now, we won't miss dessert. It's cherries Jubilee." Her heart spliced with sadness.

His expression told nothing. The smile that followed was equally ambiguous. She knew he was too proud to protest. He leaned forward and pressed his forehead against hers. "My favorite" was all he whispered.

She looked down, still frightened by the dark lure of his eyes. She saw his hands knuckle-white along the polished chintz.

WHEN COLIN RETURNED to Newport the morning of the fashion show, he found Aimee on the tennis court that, with acres of burlap, white cotton gauze and sisal rugs, had been transformed into an Arabian tent for fashion. Completing the exotic picture were a circle of swarthy, well-built men dressed only in black bow ties and black bikini swimsuits and holding long strips of black-and-white batik print cloth. In their center, Aimee was demonstrating how to wrap the cloth around their waists like a skirt. "Make sure," she instructed, tugging on the waistband of one of the men, "your sarong is secure. These ladies already have vast collections of family jewels, but give 'em a couple of Bellinis, and they could become wildcats."

Colin smiled as he watched her. She wore shapeless sweatpants and a too-big T-shirt that kept slipping off her shoulders. Her hair had been hastily pulled up and knotted. Its ends stuck out about her face in blond Statue of Liberty spikes. Her face was bare of makeup except for a bold ruby slash across her mouth. She took Colin's breath away.

"Okay, boys, let's head 'em up and move 'em out," she told her group of skirted muscle men. When she playfully patted one of the boys on his batiked bottom as he walked away, Colin chuckled. Aimee looked up, her eyes wide and alert like an animal sensing someone was near. She saw it was him and smiled. She started toward him, only some of the fear in her eyes remaining.

"Over there." She directed several men carrying in white leather modular seating. "At least fifteen feet from the end of the runway."

"Hello." She smiled and seemed unable to stop herself from taking Colin's hand in both of hers. She looked up at him with eyes round and blue as robin's eggs. "I'm so glad you're here."

He leaned down and kissed her on the cheek. His lips lingered for only a second against her soft skin. "I wouldn't have missed it for the world."

Her hands squeezed his. Then, realizing she was still holding on to him tightly, she let him go. "They predicted rain," she explained, gesturing to the transparent swags of tent ceiling. "So I decided better safe than sorry."

"The clouds are rolling in now," he confirmed. He looked around. "You've done a fantastic job."

"Really?" she answered. Excitement changed her eyes to pale blue topaz. "That's the runway there." She pointed to a long promenade rising from the middle of the sisal rugs. Taking his arm, she turned him around. "Over here we're setting up a lounge area."

Several men were arranging the modular furniture. A woman set a single belladonna lily in an Italian painted pot on one of the cube-shaped tables.

"The buffet will be served over here." Still holding his arm, she led him to one of far gauze walls. "We're having chilled oysters, grilled vegetables, swordfish sandwiches, fruit tortes."

"And your harem over there?" Colin glanced in

the direction of the bare-chested men standing and smoking just outside the tent's entrance. "I'm assuming they don't clog dance or anything?"

"They'll be serving the ladies. Most of them are fishermen Jack knows. See that one there." Aimee pointed to a man standing in the circle.

"Which one? They all look like Arnold Schwarznegger in a skirt."

"I've got some material left," Aimee said. "We could wrap you up, too."

"You don't want my chicken legs mamboing around here."

She made a face. "Are they white, too?"

"Pure paste."

She smiled. "Anyway, that Adonis there…" She pointed again to the circle. "That's Manuel Viera. He's the one who brought the fish currently seen coast to coast cradled on Vivian's lap."

"Which one? I want to shake his hand."

She pointed again. "He only came over from Portugal about three months ago. Barely speaks English. When Jack brought him to meet me, he wanted to bring me a symbol of his male prowess."

"That's what that big fish is supposed to represent? Now wait a minute. I saw that guy in a French bikini, and, like all fishermen, he's exaggerating."

"The fish was supposed to represent his fishing skill and also serve as a sort of hostess gift," Aimee explained.

Colin was still looking skeptically at the skirted males. "Continue," he said.

"*Lifestyle* was photographing Vivian on the front lawn of the house. When Jack drove up, Manuel thought Vivian was the woman he was supposed to impress. Before Jack could stop him, he jumped out of the car, ran to Vivian and laid his gift in her lap, then humbly backed away. The camera went *click,* and you know the rest. I hired Manuel immediately, of course.''

Colin was laughing, something that happened when he was around Aimee more than anyone else. ''So that's the famous fish story.''

''Just make sure it's passed down for generations to come.'' She glanced at the Rolex on Colin's wrist. ''It's that late? I've got to check on things in the dressing room and see if the caterers have come yet, and get dressed myself—''

''Whoa.'' He took both her gesturing hands in his. ''Everything's going to be fantastic. Is there anything I can do for you?''

She looked at him. He doubted she was aware of the affection in her soft blue eyes. ''I'm scared, Colin,'' she confessed in a whispery voice, as if she didn't want anyone else to hear. ''I don't suppose you could suggest any natural relaxation techniques?'' she said with a half smile.

The only natural relaxation technique Colin knew of was sex, but he wasn't going to suggest that. The poor girl was already scared enough. ''A whirlpool and warm milk?''

Her half smile became whole. ''Is that your prescription?''

''For now. But this weekend, after the show is over, and you're a great success, why don't you spend a day with me on Block Island? We'll sail over in the morning. I'll introduce you to my friends who own the Maniss Hotel, show you my own house I keep there. We can bicycle around the island, have dinner and sail back in the evening.'' He pressed her hands in his. ''Yes?''

''It sounds great,'' she admitted.

''It will be great,'' he insisted, his gaze holding hers. ''Say yes.''

She gave him a small nod. ''Yes.''

''Good girl. We'll go on Saturday, weather permitting. I'll call my friends later this week to tell them we're coming. Now let me give you a kiss for good luck.''

He kissed her on the cheek once, then again and whispered in her ear, ''If you need anything, anything at all, I'll be right inside, only a yell away. Understand?''

She nodded.

''Good.'' He gave her hands a final squeeze. ''Knock 'em dead, kid.''

He turned, making his way past the men laying wires and stringing lights. He looked back only once. Aimee still stood where he left her, her hand placed along her cheek, touching the spot where he'd kissed her.

''So...'' Hugo said, studying the game board between him and Colin. ''What do you know about Aimee Rose?''

''What do you want me to know, Hugo?'' It'd always been Hugo's preference Colin called him by his first name. Only Shawn called the old man Grandfather.

''You've asked the girl to marry you. I assume

you've looked into her background, her family, her ancestry.''

Hugo was almost completely dependent on his wheelchair now. His spirit, however, remained strong-willed and stubborn.

"Unless Shawn stops playing the court jester, which I seriously doubt, the genes of future Tremont generations to come will depend on you and your bride."

"Ironic, isn't it?" Colin moved his man on the game board, then looked his grandfather in the eye. "The bastard son giving birth to the next generation?"

Hugo studied his grandson. "Your background is mixed, Colin. There's nothing I can do to change that. It's up to you to prove you're a Tremont."

"Yes, I know. Secure the success of the company, then guarantee a generation of high-born, well-bred Tremonts."

"This isn't a matter to be treated casually." Hugo moved his game piece and captured Colin's man.

"Perhaps, but I'm marrying a woman, not a broodmare." Colin took his turn.

Hugo moved his man closer to home. "We're a privileged people. With those privileges comes responsibilities. You've always met your responsibilities before, Colin. I expect no less from you now. And you can expect no less from me than a generous reward."

"The money."

"All the money."

He had known the offer from the beginning. Had he foolishly entertained the idea of his grandfather's

approval, even dared to risk the thought of the old
man's affection? Acceptance, affection cost too
much, were too great a risk. There'd be money.
There'd always be money. And nothing else.

Colin studied the gaming table before him. He'd
thought a young boy's pain had been buried a long
time ago. He'd been wrong.

"Aimee isn't a member of the International Social
Registry, but—"

"But your family is," Hugo pointed out.

"I know she has a brother who has his own landscaping business. She worked for him and then for a
few of the boutiques in town until Vivian hired her."

Hugo's fist hit the table with surprising force considering his frail state. "That's what you know about
her—her damn résumé?"

"I know what I need to know about her. However,
I'm sure if I have her family history traced, I can
find some trivial connection to upper-class ancestry
to fulfill your narrow-minded, elitist satisfaction."

"Don't get high-handed with me, boy," Hugo
warned. "I didn't pay to save you from a life of
squalor and scandal only to see it all tumble down
around me now. The girl is lovely. When I first met
her, I thought her even suitable, but lately, her taste-
less choice in clothes and companions, plus her continuing relationship with the press has proven her of
questionable nature. I like the girl…I even defended
her when she first showed up at our dinner table
dressed as a tart, but—"

"She falls far below the Tremont standard?"
Colin provided.

"Precisely. Take my word—there's more to that girl than meets the eye."

Colin had to smile. "I won't argue with you there."

Hugo glanced up from the game board. "So the wedding's off?"

"No," Colin answered, moving his man into the safety zone.

"No?" Hugo's surprise was so genuine, Colin almost smiled.

"No," he repeated calmly. It was the first time he'd ever defied his grandfather, and they both knew it. Hugo may not love him, but he was the only family Colin had ever had. He had never before risked that tenuous relationship.

Yet even now his defiance was false. His one bold act of rebellion was to commit to a wedding that he wasn't sure would even take place. The surprise might be on both he and his grandfather on that fateful day.

He looked up at the high color of the older man's face and grew concerned. "Hugo, take my word. You've nothing to worry about."

"I'll make that decision for myself after I have your fiancée investigated."

"I know you won't take my advice but, believe me, it's not necessary."

"You're right. I won't take your advice."

"And if your investigation reveals something unsuitable about Aimee?"

The man's faded blue eyes found his grandson. "My last responsibility is to make sure this family name continues untarnished and untouchable. In our world, appearances mean more than reality. If I find incriminating information about your fiancée, information that could expose the Tremont name to scorn, and you continue to carry on with your plans of marriage, I would, without a second thought, rewrite my will.''

Colin thought of Vivian and her plan to use Aimee to secure the family fortune. He thought of his own plan to use Aimee to gain the inheritance. Finally he thought of his suspicions Aimee might be using both Vivian and himself to secure her position.

Hugo slid his last piece on the board into home. "Aha!" he cried, genuinely delighted. "I win!"

In the end, Hugo might be the only one who did win, Colin thought. It was the perfect epitaph. He looked at the smiling old man. The words were probably already engraved on the headstone.

Chapter Eleven

"Keep the bow pointed directly into the wind," Colin told Aimee. His arms came around her, his hands on hers as she gripped the helm. "Perfect. Just keep her steady while I drop the sail."

Aimee looked out to the narrow channel where too many boats already clustered. Beyond, the endless indigo of the deep water shifted. As the sweep of island shore neared, the water lightened, favoring the sky. Milky curls beckoned boats into the azure harbor. Still, Aimee knew any feelings of reassurance would be false. She'd heard the stories of the ship-eating Great Salt Pond. Even seasoned sailors cursed its shallows, its slicing cable and pipelines. Only the local divers making their living on sunken treasures praised it.

The day had dawned clear but damp. Far out from Newport Harbor, a northerly wind had come, and the white water had risen. The sails had filled, the lee rail dipping low toward the white foam. Spray wet Aimee's face. Salt stiffened her hair, coated her skin. Standing now, the steady sense of imbalance grew stronger.

Colin released the jib and ran up to the foredeck to take the sail down and tie it off against the life-lines. Then he released the main sail, furled it on the boom and secured it with ties.

He came back to where she stood. "Good job," he told her, smiling. "We'll make a sailor out of you yet."

Smiling wanly, she gratefully gave him back the helm. She walked to the stern and sat down. She leaned back, trying to relax, but the bulky lifejacket made the position feel unnatural. She sat up straight, her gaze going to Colin.

The wind combed back his hair as if the sun wanted to gaze more fully on his features. His eyes were half-closed as he concentrated on maneuvering through the thin channel into the harbor. He smiled as he steered. The engine idled in a constant hum. The sunlight danced on the boat's brass fittings.

"I left my sunglasses below." He turned to her, catching her study. He offered her his smile. "Would you mind getting them for me?"

She went down the hatchway into the cabin and found the glasses on one of the bunks. She could still feel the flush on her face when she came on deck again, and hoped it'd be mistaken for color caused by the breeze.

"Thank you," he said, accepting the glasses. He put them on and again smiled—a smile that told nothing nor took nothing. His eyes were silver mirrors.

There was a shimmering quality to the light, and the air seemed to thin. Aimee shaded her eyes and looked out to where the blue plain turned into wet, green-black rocks and boulders. Not far away, anchored schooners swayed, smaller yawls bobbed. Not a single moored vessel was still, all anxious to be away from the too-solid shore.

They'd left not long after dawn, so it was still early. Yet already the harbor was crowded. Colin maneuvered through the anchored and moored boats to a relatively remote northeast corner. "We'll pick up a mooring here," he told Aimee, pointing toward a buoy. "And use the harbor launch."

He leaned over the side of the boat and, with a big hook, picked up a rope chained to the buoy.

The harbor boat came. As Aimee stepped from one deck to another, she felt the boat they were leaving dip, then swing, already joining the others in chained dance.

Finally there was the deliverance of ground beneath her feet. The wind stayed, though, as if mocking Aimee's desire to leave the liquid roll and wallow of the water.

Colin paid the harbor fees and looked toward the marina's parking lot. "Max should've dropped off the Jeep.... There it is, over there." He gestured toward the far end of the half-filled lot.

When they reached the Jeep, he unzipped its canvas cover, exposing a square metal frame. He threw his duffel bag and Aimee's small canvas tote into the back.

"Jump in," he said, an invitation Aimee feared he meant literally until he opened the passsenger door and reached for her hand.

He fastened the seat belt around her waist and tightened it across her shoulder. She looked around the open space surrounding her. She heard the wind laugh.

He crossed the front of the Jeep and vaulted into the driver's seat. He inserted the key into the ignition, giving her a smile before putting the Jeep into gear. It was a smile of perfect joy, a smile needing no more cause or reason than the day itself. The blue sky spread behind him. The sun dazzled on the water and the white of distant sails. The universe shifted. Elements realigned. Aimee saw herself reflected in the silver mirrors of Colin's sunglasses. She was smiling.

They maneuvered the slim road leading away from the harbor inlet and headed south, past the public beaches. She wrapped her hand around a warm metal tube, a pleasant feeling of expectation and exploration overtaking her. They drove into the divine, the wild, unconscious beauty of the island a welcome contrast from Newport's stiff grandeur.

Old Harbor was only a mile away, so it was no more than minutes when they pulled into what passed as the island's center of town. Past the clapboard inns and the gray-shingled stores, Aimee saw the first ferry of the day coming toward the shore.

Colin parked and turned off the Jeep's engine. "Before we go to my house, I want to stop at the hotel and tell Max and Sheila we're here."

She nodded, exhilaration lighter than air still swelling within her. He hopped out of the Jeep and started toward her. But before he reached her, she grasped the roll bar and hurdled herself over the Jeep's side. She landed in front of Colin, her arms spread up to the sky in a gymnast's dismount. He looked down at her and laughed. "Not bad for a girl without sea legs."

"Sea legs, shoot," she said. "I can't even swim." It was an easy confession here on the island's sturdy ground.

"Except for one memorable ferry ride when I sat on the top deck and got sick from the ship's fumes," she added, "I've never sailed, either."

"I thought all Newport natives must swim and sail. Isn't it a town ordinance?" Colin teased, taking her arm and leading her toward a large Victorian structure.

"I'm not a Newport—" she started, then stopped. Colin looked down at her, his expression masked by silver mirrors.

"I don't swim or sail," was all she said.

"That's a shame considering you live on the coast. How could you live so close to the ocean and not—"

"I just didn't," she stopped him. The hard barrier of her background rose up, invisible but unshatterable, forever separating her.

Colin's silver gaze was still on her. She feared he would pursue the subject, and then what would she say?

She looked at him and saw the edge of his jaw soften.

"This hotel is beautiful," he said, changing the subject as smoothly as he led her up the front steps.

"It was built in 1870. Max and Sheila restored it exactly one hundred years later. The oak woodwork alone is worth a visit. It's all original."

He held the door open for her. He had taken off his sunglasses, and so exposed, he smiled. It was a curve of charm—not the benign flattery Shawn practiced but the magical lure of unfettered masculinity. It was a smile that promised delight, preceded danger. It took Aimee's breath.

Tomorrow, she promised. Tomorrow she would think of things unanswered and unresolved. Today she would be with Colin on this tiny island, away from the forces throwing them together and tearing them apart. It wasn't much longer, no more than a few weeks after they returned, she'd say goodbye to him. Their time together was nearly over. So they'd take today, only a few hours, and be happy.

Aimee smiled, and guided by Colin's steady, warm touch, let herself be led into the hotel, not thinking any further than each step they took together.

Max and Sheila Stein were one of those couples who'd been married so long, they finished each other's sentences. Sheila was small, dark with such a surplus of energy, she seemed to be busy even when standing still. Max was tall, lean and fair. He spoke slowly, and when he sat, he stretched himself out full-length like a river with no particular place to go.

"Let me give you the grand tour," Sheila insisted, linking her arm through Aimee's with natural hospitality. "We'll let the boys talk shop."

They passed the lounge and dining room, and Aimee was admiring the Eastlake-style bed in the first guest room when Sheila asked, "So the wedding's on?"

"What?" Aimee stiffened, the realization they

weren't so far from Newport after all as painful as if this small woman had struck her.

Sheila looked at her and began apologizing. "I'm sorry. Max always says I was born blunt."

She took Aimee's hand and gave it a pat. "Colin told us everything."

"Everything?" Aimee repeated, her mouth dry.

Sheila nodded and continued to pat her hand. "About the leak to the press, then the paparazzi hounding your every move, the rumors about your relationship with Shawn while Colin was away, Vivian's threats against *Lifestyle*. Why, it's enough to strain any young couple's commitment."

Aimee's muscles relaxed. For a paralyzing moment, she'd feared Sheila had known the truth. Colin obviously had invented this story in response to what his friends must have seen and read in the press.

"But breaking off the relationship is a little extreme, isn't it?" Sheila insisted. "Colin told me not to bring it up, but I can't believe the wedding is really off?"

"The wedding was really more other peoples' idea than ours," Aimee tried to explain.

"Well, he can't expect me to believe there's nothing between you two. He brought you here, didn't he?"

"Yes, but I don't see—"

"You're the first girl Colin has ever brought to the island."

Aimee's shock returned. "That's impossible."

"Incredible, but not impossible," the other woman insisted. "If it were otherwise, I'd know. This is a small island. There's not much to do in the off-season except catch up on the local gossip.''

Aimee didn't know what to say. She stood there, staring at this small, dark woman. She felt surprise still solid on her features.

"That's why it's so hard for me to believe everything's over between you two," Sheila continued. "You must be very special to Colin if he brought you here."

She was definitely *special* to Colin, Aimee agreed, but not in the way this woman assumed. She wondered what the hotel owner would say if she knew the truth about her relationship with Colin and the rest of the Tremont clan? The story would probably provide enough entertainment to sustain the locals through the long winter and sleepy spring.

"I asked him once why he never brought anyone here." Sheila smoothed the bed's quilted corner. "All he said was the only worthwhile woman in the world was already married to his friend Max. He was teasing me, of course." Still, the older woman's eyes shone, and Aimee could see she'd been the rare object of Colin's commanding charms.

"The way I always figured it," Sheila speculated as she guided Aimee to the next room, "is that the island, like it is for most of the cottagers, is Colin's sanctuary. His life here is so different from the life he leads when away from here, he wants to keep the two worlds separate." She looked at Aimee. "At least he did until now."

Sheila stopped beneath a nineteenth-century illustration. "He's a good man and a good friend," she said, searching Aimee's eyes. "But beyond the island, any love he's been given, he's been given grudgingly. It can make a man hard toward the world.''

Aimee looked down at her hostess. ''He has been a good friend to me, Sheila…and I've tried to be a friend to him, too. We're friends, that's all.''

''That's nice,'' Sheila said, the words drawled out as her lips curled up into a pixie's smile. She looked at Aimee as if they were partners on an inside joke.

They found the men in one of the guest rooms, inspecting several long scratches grooved into the woodwork. Like the others, the room charmed the eye with its period furnishings. The rug was thick beneath its guests' feet. The dresser top was solid marble. Candles, fresh flowers and a decanter of brandy surrounded by snifters completed the room's appeal.

''Did you say some of the ones in the other rooms are even worse?'' Colin asked. He ran a fingertip across a deep scratch.

''Afraid so,'' Max answered.

Colin shook his head. His finger stroked the wood like a parent trying to heal a child's wound. ''The whole piece should be taken off, sanded smooth, restained and repolyed. Staining isolated pieces, however, will probably result in shade differences.''

''Are you saying refinish all the woodwork again?'' Max rubbed his hand across his forehead.

Colin nodded. ''And urethane every piece with that acrylic poly they use on gymnasium floors.''

Max shook his head. ''The cost aside, which makes me glad Sheila reminded me to take my blood pressure pill this morning, we're in the middle of the season.''

Colin straightened but still looked at the damaged molding. ''We might be able to fill in the marks, then blend them with a touch-up pencil. It'll be a patch job, but it'll get you through the season.''

''I always said you were a saint. Didn't I always tell you that?''

Colin smiled at his friend. ''No.''

''Yes, I did,'' Max insisted. ''Saint Colin, that's what I call you.''

''Don't start canonizing me yet,'' Colin cautioned. ''Let me do a little experimenting first to make sure we can match the color.''

He squatted back down to examine the scratches once again. ''I could even show you how to fix the trim yourself so it's done right this time.''

''And without labor costs,'' Max added, a smile in his voice. ''When you come back in the winter, you'll stay right here, and we'll make a party of it.''

Colin stood up. ''I may not be around this winter.''

''What do you mean you're not going to be around this winter?'' Sheila demanded. ''You always come in the off-season and spend time with us.''

The way Colin's head jerked toward the women, Aimee realized he'd been so engrossed in his study of the woodwork, he hadn't heard them come in.

''Where will you be? Sailing around the world?''

His expression eased into a smile. ''In a way. I'm scheduled to travel to several foreign countries to select new sites for the stores. Next year we begin the first phase of our overseas expansion.''

"Work, work, work," Sheila scolded. "I prefer my guests. Haven't I always wanted to go around the world?" she asked her husband.

"Just get on a boat and sail east," she rambled on, not waiting for an answer. "I know a couple who did that for their honeymoon. Isn't that romantic?" She now turned to Aimee. "Isn't that the perfect honeymoon?"

Max rolled his eyes, but when his gaze leveled once more, he looked at his wife lovingly. "Are you starting already? I'm going to ask the surgeon general when he stays here in August to print a warning on your backside. *Please be advised—coming within ten feet may be hazardous to your single status.*"

He looked at Aimee. "You'll have to excuse my wife. She likes to play matchmaker. I'm sure Colin's used to it by now."

"Can I help it if I find marriage a blissful state of being?" His wife smiled at him, a young girl's features reborn in her face.

Max walked to her side, putting his arm around her. "Thanks, love, but be a peach and lay off our dear friend here and his guest." He looked at Aimee once again. "She's made it her personal crusade to see Colin married. The morning of his wedding, she'll be the one crying the hardest."

Aimee thought of her plan to thwart Vivian. "Not if Vivian is there," she remarked, the words leaving her mouth before she could stop them.

In the second of silence that followed, she suffered Colin's sharp glance and the Steins' puzzled gazes.

"Vivian?" Sheila asked, her dislike of the woman evident.

Aimee laughed lightly, easing out of the awkward quiet. "She doesn't exactly come across as the sentimental type, does she?"

Sheila opened her mouth but before she could offer an opinion, Max interceded. "Enough already with the wedding talk. If you want to see tears, I'll show you the electric bill that arrived this morning. Now, come on, let's eat."

Sheila rolled her eyes. "Talk about your sentimental types…"

Max linked his arm through his wife's. "I'm as sentimental as the next guy…when my belly's full."

"I rest my case," she said.

"Good, because the best breakfast buffet on the island is waiting on the deck of the 1661 Inn across the street." He checked his watch. "If we didn't miss it already."

His wife patted his arm. "You're the owner, remember? I'm sure we can get served."

"Shh," he said in a stage whisper. "I was going to impress Aimee by telling her I'm buying."

Aimee laughed and started to follow her hosts when she was stayed by Colin's hand on her arm.

"You two go on ahead," he told his friends. "We'll catch up in a minute."

Aimee saw Sheila look at Max. They didn't say a word. They didn't have to. She knew what they were thinking by the looks that passed between the couple. *Young love,* their eyes silently conveyed.

"Nice save." Colin's voice came to her, remote and close at the same time. She knew he was talking about her earlier offhand remark.

"I'm sorry—"

"There's no need to apologize. I'm sure you got the third-degree drill from Sheila already during the tour."

Aimee smiled. "She doesn't believe a thing you told her about canceling the wedding."

"I had to tell her something or she'd be organizing a his-and-hers shower right now," Colin explained.

"I don't think it worked. She's convinced we're getting married. She said I was the first woman you ever brought to the island."

"You are," he confirmed.

Aimee felt again the rush of surprise. Beneath its dizzying drag, she felt a forbidden breath of pleasure.

"Why?"

"Because you're different," he said without expression, without expectation.

He started toward the door, physically moving away from the subject. "Let's go eat," he said, then stopped. He looked back at her.

"Will you be crying the morning of our wedding day?" he asked.

"We're not getting married," she reminded him.

"Will you be crying?" he asked again.

Yes, her heart thought.

"No," she said aloud. This time she was the first to start from the room.

After breakfast, they climbed back in the Jeep and headed to the west side of the island. Aimee concentrated on the passing hills edged with low stone walls and wiry brush. The wind had grown stronger. It careened and danced around her like a dervish. It tangled her hair and caught at her breath. Colin tapped her on the shoulder, pointed toward the hills and said something, but his words were carried away by the breeze. He moved his mouth like a player in a silent movie, the absence of sound causing Aimee to be struck by the raw, uneven beauty of his face, not unlike this island he so loved. She turned away. The green hills seemed to vibrate across the horizon.

Colin turned the Jeep sharply down a sloping dirt road. Kicking stones, the vehicle continued until it came to a gray-shingled Victorian nestled down, hiding from the island's constant breeze. Weathered wicker chairs faced the sea on each side of the front porch. Dandelions nodded in the new sprung grass. The large shed out back was the same worn gray as the house.

"Here we are," Colin announced. He got out of the Jeep and reached for their bags in the back. Aimee had packed only a swimsuit, sunscreen, hairbrush, tinted lip balm and a sweatshirt. She was dressed in twill shorts and a V-necked T-shirt, her hair a single braid down her back. Her alter ego of flamboyant clothes and dramatic makeup had been left behind in Newport. She felt light, free as if she could fly on this ever-present Block Island breeze.

She reached for the tote.

"I've got it," Colin assured her, already leading the way to the house.

The screen door slammed behind them as they entered. "Here we are." Colin set down her bag on a caned bench in the foyer. To the right of the staircase, she could see a book-lined study, to the left, a living room.

He motioned her to follow him. They passed through the living room to the kitchen. A door off the kitchen was opened to a dining room. The rooms were high-ceiling and united by polished, wide-planked floors. The furniture was simple, the windows wide and curtainless. The light, so sought, came and shone on the floors and walls and the beautiful woodwork borders between them.

"Bellevue Avenue it ain't," Colin said.

"It's better," she said. Stark, simple and strong, it spoke of the man who created it. After the pomp of Newport, it was a restful breath. She walked to the kitchen's bay window seat and stood in the curve of light.

She heard Colin approaching, and she glanced over her shoulder. He was smiling. "You should see it in the wintertime," he said, stepping into the sun and standing beside her. "The lee shore sleeps then. The houses are shuttered. The light is so raw, shadows become substance."

They stood there for a stopped moment, Colin in a midwinter's dream and Aimee, the newcomer, already content. The feeling of imbalance begun in the water had never abated, but no longer was its effect merely frightening. It brought others' words to her in a rhythm of song. She could feel the sway of her body as if being rocked gently on the brink.

"That's my workshop," Colin said, awakening, his tone too efficient. He was speaking of the low building framed by the kitchen's tall windows. "I told Max, if there was time, I'd try to match the stain on the wood sample he gave me from the hotel. Do you mind?"

"Not at all. I'll sit right there." Aimee's gaze was

on the swath of sunlight silvering the dune grasses.
"And rest."

THE LENGTH of her stretched out across a wicker
chaise, her pulse slowed by the sun. Colin had
dragged out a bench from the workshop and sat several yards away. He worked in the shade, so the heat
wouldn't thicken the stain. Aimee's sunglasses further tinted the world around him as she watched him
work.

Even without her sunglasses, she doubted he
would've noticed her study. Through the glasses'
colored windows casting all images unreal, she saw
the man she'd glimpsed before, then was gone. Bend-
ing toward his work, the ever-present tilt of his jaw
had dropped, and his mouth, opened, was smiling
unconsciously. The scornful lines of his face eased;
his body's rigid posture released. He was no longer
the spiring mast but the bellying sail. She had
thought it was the wood that had solely born this
man, but she now knew it was also the wind. She,
too, felt the lift of the current, the lightening of the
spirit.

He stared hard at the wood as if seeking its secrets,
then dipped a foam brush into a small, opened can
and dabbed at the piece. He waited, patient, tranquil,
watching the color dry. A triumphant light came into
his eyes, and his smile widened.

He stood and came to her, the wood still in his
hand as if he didn't want to let it go. He stood over
her, backlit by the sun, the breeze curling the longer
lengths of his hair.

"I've found a good match. Let me clean up, and

we'll go for a bike ride." He looked out, squinting at the sea. "Before the wind becomes much stronger."

"Please don't rush on my account." Aimee stretched out even longer, her muscles loosened by the warmth. "I'm completely content."

His gaze had come back to her. With the wind washing over them like waves, she looked up into his eyes.

He sat down on the end of the lounge chair beside her crossed calves. The sun returned, splaying across them. The teetering sensation became stronger.

The man she'd seen come, soothed by the air's spirits and the wood's substance, remained. For the moment, chilling composure, angry asides, even suspect smiles were gone, forgotten.

"I'm glad I brought you here," he said. He didn't touch her. He didn't need to.

She felt the sun on her skin, conscious of the areas of her body bare and exposed. She felt her vulnerability. She felt his.

He stood back up, the withdrawal of his weight rolling her body toward him. The seesaw sensation inside her never stopped.

"I'll be right back," he said.

She watched him gather his tools and take them inside the workshop. He went into the house and emerged. His hair was wet and shiny black, combed off his forehead; his face was freshly washed, revealed. As he crossed the spiky grass, he held out his hands for the sun to dry the last remaining drops of water. Then he offered one hand to her.

"Ready?"

She put her hand in his, letting him pull her up.

"Ready," she said. A breath of island breeze came, caught her word and carried it away.

Chapter Twelve

"Which way first? North? South?" Colin asked as Aimee coasted to a stop beside him. The metallic finish of their bikes sparkled in the sun.

She tilted the bike and balanced on one foot as she looked up and down the road. "What do you think?"

"The ride south is much more uphill, especially when you near the bluffs. We should go that way while we're still fresh."

"Sounds good to me," she agreed.

They righted their bikes and started toward the southern coast. Spare, dirt paths crisscrossed the asphalt road. To their left, Colin pointed out the ravine of Rodman's Hollow, one of the island's five wildlife refuges. The path climbed and dipped, the sea's wavy surface continued in the island's sloping green hills. Stone walls and dry squares of brush split the landscape. Victorian houses, always turned toward the sea, gathered at the base of the hills.

They parked their bikes on the Mohegan Trail and walked down a short, sandy trail leading to the bluffs. At the end of the path, they stood on reddish clay cliffs two hundred feet high. A wooden stairway led to a rocky strip of beach below and the boundless blue Atlantic.

"It's beautiful," Aimee said, standing high on the precipice.

"Do you see that there?" Colin shouted against the gathering wind. He pointed left to a brick gingerbread-house structure perched above the sea. "That's the Southeast Light. It was built in the 1870s, and still flashes today."

Aimee turned toward the lighthouse, the wind without boundaries blowing, unweaving her hair from its braid.

"Do you want to go down to the beach?" Colin pointed toward the wooden stairs.

She nodded, smoothing back loosened strands of hair from her face. The wind cackled and curled them forward again.

Colin took her hand, pulling her close to him as they walked toward the stairs.

The wind rose in a fury as they descended to the rocky beach. The gulls' cries seemed wilder. Colin's arm went around her shoulder, pulling her even closer, his body a buffer against the currents swirling in from the sea. His other hand still held hers, steadying her as they crossed the stony shore.

Beneath her, she could feel the hardness of the rocks. Beside her, she could feel the hardness of the man holding her, not letting her go. Their bodies touched, buoyed by the wind. Talk would be too loud and swallowed swiftly by the breeze. Touch became their communication.

She walked with him and the wind and the sea and sometime splash of sun, her defenses wearing smooth as the stones stripped by the sea, her desire rising like the tide.

They stopped at a curve in the cliff wall big enough to shelter two people. Still the wind found them, whipping Aimee's hair across her face. Colin smoothed it back from her temples. She felt the dryness of his skin, the tenderness of his touch. In the darkness of his eyes she saw her own desire.

She leaned against the cliff wall, still beneath the buffer of his arm. There were no sounds but the wind and the wail of the gulls. Before them were only the sea and the sky, a world simple and removed.

The rocks were cool against Aimee's back. Colin's lips, kissed by the wind, were cool as they touched the spot of her neck curving toward him. The wait, begun long before this moment, had so bound her muscles, her body went limp. His own body caught her, curving, then straightening, supporting her with a slow slide of muscles, pushing her back against the rocks, holding fast her liquid form.

His mouth once more pressed open against her neck. Her head bent to his, her brow resting on his crown. Her hand opened, laid soft against the hard curve of his cheek. His mouth, open, hungry, moved toward hers in a glide of lips and skin. Her body, full against his, moved in a long shiver. Her head dipped, taking those tortuous lips for her own. Her tongue shot out, then slowly withdrew, both bodies shuddering now and muscles, once weak, taut as strung wire.

With kisses she tasted the sea air on his skin. With silken touches she felt the cool cling of the wind on his body. Beyond him, the breaking waves began to rise higher. She closed her eyes, no longer caring why he wanted her. He wanted her. She wanted him. Without reason.

She curved around him, kissing him openmouthed, taking the tongue he offered and stroking, suckling it with her own. She pressed her hips to his, the deep need inside her too great. She was conscious of her movements, even shocked, but she wouldn't stop. The wanting was too real, the need too thick.

He kissed her mouth, her neck, the V of tender skin above her breasts. His hand gently cupped the heavy weight of one breast. Her breath answered in a soft sigh of relief.

His thumb brushed her erect nipple, the shocking sweetness of his touch sending her senses spinning. She went soft in his arms, knowing nothing but this man and the clench of frenzied wind surrounding them.

"Colin," she said, her voice thick, calling.

It was the sound of his name, her voice blending with the wind, that drew him back from the sweet pull of her. The brash smell of sea salt filled his nostrils, and the air was crystalline. The cliff wall stood bold and chiseled. The rimming meadow grasses were slim as sabers. Where everything should have been soft and fluid, he found vigilant reality. Fear, impaling and razor-real, cut through his consciousness.

He stepped farther back from her. The wind rushed in with a cruel caress. He held her by the shoulders. Her eyes looked up at him, glazed and brilliant blue.

This was no longer a charade, a burlesque performed for amusement and advantage. If he made love to her now, he'd be hers. All would be lost.

"Colin?" She said his name hesitantly. So quickly a cry of desire became a question.

Still, he drew her to him, pressing her beautiful, bewildered face to his heartbeat. He couldn't let her go; yet he couldn't take her now. Later, when control came back, and passion was remembered as the flames of a fatal crash.

He schooled his features into a fortress, aligned his body and prayed the desire didn't still burn black in his eyes.

"I apologize, Aimee." He cursed himself when his voice uttered her name like a soft benediction.

He breathed and began again. She had sensed the steeling of his body and had stepped back, out of his embrace. He would've thought it'd be easier when he wasn't touching her. It was worse. The leading muscles of his arm twitched as if to reach out and gather her close once more. He locked his shoulders, curled his fingers.

"I've been direct about my affection for you, and you've been equally honest about your lack of similar feelings for me. I accepted and respected your position, and offered you friendship, a partnership."

His voice was pure New England bred—all remote, elongated *A*s.

"But if I'd been honest with you—and myself— we would have known before now, I entered into this friendship with an ulterior aim."

She had backed up to the cliff wall. Her body had hardened as if to blend with the rocks.

"I see now, as I must confess to you, I offered

friendship in the hopes of increasing your affection for me. Although I've been restrained in your presence in the past, my actions just now force me to realize seduction must've been my secret motive behind our sail here today.''

He heard his speech—formal, pompous, another necessary defense against the desire ringing his soul.

"The fact this seduction was spontaneous and only subconsciously anticipated doesn't excuse my behavior. I know the situation and your unusual position within the family, and I congratulate you on your ability to realize a relationship between us would be complicated.''

He saw his speech begin to soften her. Her rigid posture relaxed enough so it was clear where cool, carved rock ended and the yield of her skin began. She wrapped her arms across her chest, hugging herself.

"So I end as I began—with an apology.'' He didn't offer his hand, knowing one touch, and all his carefully clung-to reason would scatter.

He waited for her reaction, wondering if she was weighing her choices, debating the odds. Vivian had assured her a million dollars along with the family fortune for her marriage to Shawn and her false attraction to himself. Vivian had also initiated Aimee's entrance into the world of fashion, a door which would be swiftly and permanently shut if her protégée didn't fulfill her half of the bargain.

So far, he'd offered her nothing but himself.

The choice was obvious. The ardor he'd imagined in her kisses, her touch, must've been merely a reflection of his own needs.

Needs that still rose high as if an unchangeable tide. Desire stayed, but to it was added anger. Anger at how easily he'd been manipulated.

He wouldn't wait for her words. He couldn't tell what was true, what was false in his own words. How could he tell in hers? The only truth now, the only reality was his desire. Beyond that, all else blurred.

He saw her mouth open, but he raised his hand, halting her speech. "We should go if we want to see the North Light." He was controlled, commanding. She looked at him, eyes dazed, confused, but she didn't protest. She didn't say anything.

He led the way back, pausing at the steps to let her go first. He didn't take her hand. The space was narrow, and as she moved by him, he saw she was holding her breath, contracting her muscles as if afraid to accidentally touch him. He stood, turned toward her but looked beyond her to where the ocean met the sky.

"We'd better head back to the house," he said.

She stopped two steps above and turned.

"See those clouds out there?"

He pointed at a mass of tarnished gray moving in slow motion toward them. He looked at her for the first time since they started back. "A storm is coming."

"A storm?" Her eyes were as somber as the coming clouds.

"Storms hit quickly on the island, but, just as quickly, can pass." He spoke in a calming tone.

"How long will this one last?"

He looked to the sea. The waves were gathering strength, breaking against the shore in a shattering release of power. The wind was high, anguished. "It depends on the storm."

He turned from the sea and took a step up the stairs. "As long as you're on land, you're safe."

Her eyes were even with his, and he could see they both knew he was lying.

She turned away from him and started up the stairs. Desire coiled at the base of his spine. The first raindrop fell.

THEY WERE SOAKED by the time they reached the house. They had pedaled hard and fast, trying to stay ahead of the heavy rain. When they finally stopped, their breaths came in partnered pants.

"You get in the house," Colin yelled above the wind. "I'm going down to the marina to make sure the boat's secure."

He started toward the barn with the bikes. "Whoa!" he cried as the wind tried to push him back. She heard the unexpected challenge of his laugh above the wind. "She's a wild one."

Standing at a curtainless front window, she watched him drive off in the shelter of the canvas-covered Jeep. She watched until there was nothing but puddles rippling from the car wheels.

She found a towel in the upstairs bathroom, unfastened her braid and dried her hair. A terry-cloth robe hung on the back of the door. She peeled off her wet clothes and wrapped herself in the robe. It swallowed her up, making her slight body look even smaller. She wiped away the smears of mascara around her eyes and finger combed the tangles in her hair. The braid had thickened her hair into waves.

She had started a pot of coffee and was sitting at the end of the kitchen's long trestle table when Colin came in. He slammed the back door, shutting out the wind and rain. He shook his head, spraying drops of water that darkened the wood floor. He ran his hands through his hair, slicking it back off his brow. His features, unrelieved and polished with rain, increased their domination.

His soaked shirt clung to his chest, outlining the muscular relief beneath. His pants wrapped in wet sheaths around the long, hard length of his limbs. Aimee remembered him naked the first night she'd spent in the Tremont mansion. She felt her own nakedness beneath the robe. She couldn't look at him any longer. She stood and went to the counter, pretending to check the coffeepot.

"The boat'll hold," he said. "I feel sorry, though, for the poor fools who rafted an entire flotilla on one anchor. The storm will send them sailing off to sea with one strong swoop. But who knew we'd get hit so quickly? They've already closed the airstrip and canceled the ferries. We'll just have to sit tight and let Mother Nature have her way with us."

She heard his unexpected, throaty laughter again and realized the pure physical force of the wind and the rain had lessened his tension.

"Where are the coffee cups?" she asked, turning to him. He was unbuttoning his shirt.

"The cupboard to your left."

He stripped off the shirt. A raindrop fell from his hair to his shoulder. Aimee watched it move slowly across the curve of his collarbone, down smooth, coppery skin, baptizing marble muscles.

"I'm going upstairs to change. You probably need some clothes, too."

"Anything in a size seven will do." She smiled, pleased with the nonchalant tone in her voice.

He smiled back. His teeth were white, his hair wet black, his skin brown. There were no shadows or silhouettes. His form was as clear and contrasting as a printer's plate. "The only thing I have in a size seven is a hat."

Aimee, still struggling to stay afloat, answered, "I'll need more than that."

He nodded. Despite his etched form, the thoughts behind those hewn features remained unknown.

He folded his arms across his bare chest as if putting up an additional barrier. His forearms were thick—his upper arms swells of muscle, but his fingers were long and slender. *Tremont hands,* Aimee thought.

"Let me see what I can find," he said.

She heard him climb the stairs. With each step he took, she could feel thigh muscles lengthen, contract. She stood up and went to the kitchen counter. She took two cups out of the cupboard and placed them next to the coffeepot. His footsteps were over her head now. She heard the creak of the floorboards above.

He could've had her on the beach. Her hands gripped the cool steel edge of the sink. He could have her now.

THE PHONE LINES were down. The electricity went out an hour later. Colin lit oil lamps, and Aimee made peanut butter sandwiches. Afterward, they sat and played rummy, sometimes talking, sometimes concentrating too hard on the spread of cards in their hands. The storm moaned outside; a constant current thrummed inside. Neither knew what time it was when Aimee stretched her body long and said goodnight. They both knew, however, sleep wouldn't come easily.

Aimee unfolded a checked blanket across her body and lay back in the high brass bed. The rain fell hard on the roof above. Her heart beat to its tempo. The blackness around her gradually lessened and took on form.

She didn't want to think. She wanted to sleep. She rolled and burrowed her body, but only thoughts came. Sleep did not.

The rain washed the world, and Aimee thought of right and wrong and risk. A quarter hour. A half hour. The moon watched the restless twists of her body. The wind sang her discontent. Her heart beat for another.

She heard the floorboards creak, wondering if it was another's impatient pace or only the night's noises? Did Colin sleep or suffer as she did, her body curled tight and her hair moist against her nape.

This afternoon, when the kiss had become a wet, full draw of lips and tongue, and they'd met, body to body, the blood desperately rushing, his hands full of her, her fingers pressed into his flesh, she wished he'd hadn't pulled away. She wished he'd made the choice for him, for her. She knew he wanted her. He'd told her long ago, but there'd been no force, no plea, no coax. Only respect, friendship.

Where a wild, rare happiness grew.

Since the beginning, he'd given the choice to her. It was hers. It'd always been hers. He'd waited. He waited still.

The bed was high. It seemed to take a long time for her feet to reach the floor. She didn't reach for a robe, and the floorboards were cool as she padded barefoot across the room and down the stairs. Everything was dark. The windows were silver and radiant with rain.

She continued through the kitchen, her steps surprisingly surefooted. She walked, not hesitating once, out the back door into the wind and the rain. She went to the long, low barn, knowing long before she saw the flicker of the oil lamp in the far corner that she'd find Colin inside.

The wind announced her, and he looked up from the woodwork. She wore only an oversize white T-shirt that fell to her knees, and her hair was still fat and ripply from its earlier wet weave. In the shadowy light, she was no more than a spirit. Otherworldliness fell on Colin, too, silhouetted in the old-fashioned light, wonder in his eyes.

Aimee looked at this man, and her heart lifted. Despite the wind's pleas and the body's torment, this afternoon wasn't their time. Nor was anytime before. Right now, in the center of the storm, their time had come. She stepped toward him.

Colin's hand tightened on the wood, felt the pulse of its veins, its marrowed surface. He could feel the piece beneath his touch, smell it, raise it to his mouth and taste it if the desire overcame him. The wood was real.

The woman was not. She stood, a specter with the

black of the storm and the wind roiling behind her
and the brilliance of the sea in her eyes. There was
nothing tangible to cling to. Bodies were too pliant.
Hearts were too tender. Feelings brittle. She stood,
swimming in waters of what if and why not.

She moved. Like the wind, the air, a sweet sigh.
Coming here she had nothing to gain, not anything
more than she'd already been guaranteed. Yet, still
she came toward him, her steps small but unbroken.
She came close, an offering. He breathed her in, loosened his lips and inhaled until the wonder of her, the
very unreality of her flowed from his brain, down his
limbs, a cleansing current. She came to him. He
opened his arms. She silently slid into them.

Their first touches were light, fingertips to forearms, the skimming of skin. Hands fluttered, took
flight, then alighted again, learning firm edges, fallen
recesses. In contrast, their desire was hard, gripping,
clutching them so they shook. Still, almost maddeningly perverse, their touches were mere brushes and
wings. As if already loathing the end, they were ten-
tative to begin.

Then, senses elevated to the edge, he pulled her to
him. The rail of his ribs was beneath her palms; her
head fit into the curve of his throat. She breathed into
its hollow. Her chin lifted, and she flattened her body
to his. Their first kiss, long, slow, seeking, brought
in the blackness and the riotous wind. She clung to
his shoulders, holding on.

He fell to his knees, wrapping his arms around her
waist, pressing his face to the swell of her stomach.
Heat gathered underneath.

She bowed and curved herself around him, her hair

shrouding them. Her hands ran down his back, finding strength, resistance. She kneeled down, seeking his eyes. Their gazes level, she touched his mouth. "Make love to me," she whispered.

He picked her up and carried her to the house. She didn't feel the wind or the rain on her body. All she knew was a yearning that receded the world. He laid her on the cushioned sofa in the curtainless living room and stripped the T-shirt off her body, leaving her naked before him except for white cotton panties. He took a long, indrawn breath. The same shudder passed through her body. She looked down and saw her body, young and ripe. Her thighs had parted, greedy. She stretched her arms up to him.

He leaned over her, bracing himself, his hands locking on her wrists. He began at her mouth, only his lips and tongue touching her. He nibbled, nuzzled, his tongue probing and pleasing. As he began to move down her neck, her own head lifted, trying to stay close to his touch. His mouth covered her nipple. She felt her lower body twist. She pleaded for more, unashamed.

He licked her swollen tip with the lightest of touches, fine-tuning the tremble in her body. He moved from one taut bud to the other, tasting, savoring, until her body arched upward, seeking him. Still his body stayed suspended above her, just beyond her reach. The heat between her thighs became heavy. Her hips lifted. Sensation spread throughout her like white noise.

The tip of his tongue scored the yield of her abdomen. Her pelvis rose to meet him. Her blood became oil. His hands still wrapped around her wrists, he opened his mouth against the cloth covering the center of her desire. He parted his lips wider, his tongue licking, his teeth pressing against the white sheath until her hips began to rock faster, and her breath came through clamped teeth.

He released her wrists. Her hands reached for him, but he'd sat back on his haunches and was sliding her panties down her thighs. Then his hands held her hips and lifted her, hot and moist, to his mouth. The tip of his tongue touched her once, twice, then a third, long, sleek slide, and she was screaming, her head tipped back too far, the physical boundaries of her body broken. She was no more than pulsing light and color. Laughing, she fell weightless like the wind, her world red and sheer sensation.

Slowly, reluctantly, she came back. She was still smiling. Tiny aftershocks tensed her hips. Eyes closed, she stretched her body, feeling each muscle ripple, then constrict. She opened her eyes, amused by the rise and fall of her breasts. She looked up and met Colin's eyes. Her greed returned.

She reached for his hand and pressed it against the slick, hot sweetness of her. She rose and put her mouth to his, her sex, moving, rubbing against his palm. Her tongue thrust into his mouth, the lush moistness found there tasting of fertile spring. Her body—bones dissolved, muscles jelled—melted itself across the man, lowering him to the soft cushions.

She rose up, all fours above him, and began to unbutton his shirt, pausing at each new square of exposed skin to take a caressing taste. Her lips circled and feathered across and up and down. His hands tangled in her hair. She explored the ridges of his rib cage. She traced the fine line of black hair disappearing into his jeans, smiling as his stomach muscles sucked tight.

She unbuckled his belt, unzipped his pants, releasing him, and all became softness and hardness and long, low moans.

Her mouth caressed its way back up his body until she lay full on the length of him. His hands cupped her face, bringing her mouth to his and kissing her with the fierceness that'd taken them both. Kissing her again and again so that her breath grew short and the words she whispered were husky and begging.

He rolled her over, beneath him, his body wrapped around hers. She reached for him and slid him inside her, filling her, her thigh muscles tensing with pleasure. He moved slowly in and out, watching her. Then his arms tightened around her, carrying her with him. The movements became hard, fast, desperate. They climaxed, their cries anguished and hoarse and grateful. She heard a wild whoop of male laughter, and opened her eyes to see Colin above her, his face angled to the sky, youthful, smiling, diamond bright. There was no furrowed brows or wary glances. There was no motives, no matters of marriage or money. There was nothing but a man and a woman…and complete joy.

COLIN LOOSENED the lines. The main sail bellied, the lee rail dropped, and the sloop lifted like a bird trying to fly. He walked to the bow and sat. The day, washed by the storm, was blue edged and brilliant. Other white sails, unfurled by the new breeze, shimmied across the sea. Long, lean clouds bleached the sky. The woman, turning brown on the teak deck, slept, her storm spent.

Last night they'd made their way up to his narrow bedroom, their bodies craving even as their limbs still trembled. They'd made love on the wide gold floorboards, then staggered to the bed and clung to each other in the fold of the high, feathered mattress. They fell into sleep until the fierceness woke them once more. Night turned to morning. They woke to a high sun. The storm was over. Timelessness had ceased.

He looked at the lady, knowing the desire that lay beneath that still exterior, the desire that lay in wait within him. Even now, in the bright sun, he didn't know what was real and what was not, what should be feared and what should be embraced, exalted. He had relinquished control.

"Aimee?" he said.

She felt her arms and legs become long, blending with the movement of the sea. Her skin's binds dissolved beneath the hypnotic sun, and she was no more than the wave of the water, the roll of the wind. Beneath her closed eyes, the light was starred and the world peaceful.

She drifted, letting her thoughts have no more weight than the sunlight on her closed lids. She could still hear the words murmured and the soft laughter meeting. She could still feel lightning pleasure, the long, slow descent and swoop of desire. She allowed herself to feel her love for Colin full and fantastic on her soul. She allowed her thoughts to go no further.

She stretched, her arms spreading to the sun, her very marrow melted warmth. She knew she wasn't dreaming, but still she didn't want to wake.

"Aimee?" She heard Colin say her name, and now was anxious to open her eyes. Lifting her body into a feline curve, she sat up and looked.

On the horizon was Newport.

Chapter Thirteen

"Marry me."

Aimee's head pulled up. The noon sun gilded her gaze. Outlined against the gold foil was Colin.

He sat down next to her on the marble bench and his features took form, the gold dazzle challenged by the unbroken black of his hair, the deepened bronze of his skin.

He loves me, she thought, and went giddy. Since returning from the island, there'd been touches, looks, light public kisses more real than artifice. Still, she knew her perceptions were colored by her own deep emotion for this man. In the night, when thoughts dismissed during the day returned, she couldn't help but wonder if she'd become the biggest victim of her own pretense.

But no, she thought, relief and happiness ballooning, doubts dissolving. *He wants to marry me. Marry me.* The words had been his; now they were hers.

She loved him. She'd not said it—not yet. Nor had he. Too much had come before to rush into low pledges, hasty utterances. Even as the feeling grew, was given wings to fill her from head to heart to soul, she stayed silent, shy, waiting.

Now she would wait no more. Her love had been given voice, would become soft devotions, brash declarations. She feared nothing. All that'd come before and all that was to come after would stumble and fall before this love; this love that never should've been, but was born anyway between two hearts.

She loved him. She would tell him now. He loved her. She knew it as certainly as if they were the next words he would speak.

Her mouth opened.

His mouth opened.

She closed her lips in a smile, urging him to speak first.

"I understand the original agreement was for you to marry Shawn, and I'm aware you've been guaranteed several incentives by Vivian to ensure that end," he said.

He paused, but his black gaze on her was steady.

"At this time I'm not in a position to duplicate those terms, but I can offer you something equally enticing."

A buzzing began in her ears. Colin's words came to her as if unreal.

"Many department stores now offer their own house brands as an affordable alternative for customers. Leonard's began as a men's store, but added a women's department in the late 1960s. In the early eighties, we opened an entire women's store adjacent to our original site. None of the old-timers will admit it, but in some ways, our women's sales have been more successful than our men's. In fact, more than half the space in any of our new stores is now given over to women's retailing.''

She heard Colin's words above the ringing in her ear. She tasted the words of love halted halfway up her throat, thick, gagging.

"The time is now right for Leonard's to offer its own women's line, from business wear to sportswear to evening wear. These private-label goods would be sold in Leonard's, of course, but also be made available to competitors like Macy's and Bloomie's.''

Colin paused again. She liked to think he needed a long infusion of breath, but he showed no such frailty. Such declarations of love, she thought, the silvery ringing in her ears and a desire to laugh madly stopped only by her own avowals thickening in her throat.

"I can offer you the position of head designer of Leonard's personal label.''

He could stare directly into her eyes. His control, his mastery of emotion was consummate.

"Marry me.''

The clot in Aimee's throat was round as Florida oranges shipped north at Christmastime. Her insides felt dry, bleached. Anger tried to push past the full fist in her throat. The high ringing in her ears didn't stop.

She wanted water, not to drink but to dissolve in. She wanted the sea, to wade out to where the blue turned green. There she'd rest. She'd lay back and let the water carry her until her nerve endings turned numb, and she could forget, forget.

Oh, Colin, the cry came from deep down inside

her, *you didn't have to offer me anything. My love asked for nothing. My heart was given freely. The only thing I wanted was you.*

He was waiting for her reply, the black holes of his eyes watching.

"I want a five-year contract," she said with an almost admirable matter-of-factness.

Not the tiniest movement of muscle altered his expression. So efficient, so unflinching was his emotion, she felt the first crack in her own control, the surge of screaming anger, the writhe of unrefined pain.

"Business contract or marriage contract?" he asked, continuing the practical tone.

Useless, unspoken cries came from her heart. *Come back, Colin,* they murmured. *My Colin of the wind and the rain and the smiles. Come home.*

"Is there a difference?" she asked.

There wasn't even a wry smile. "It seems not."

She picked up the mechanical pencil that'd rolled into her lap and resumed her sketching. She couldn't look at him anymore. "The date is two weeks from this Saturday."

"I'll return the Friday before. Until then I'll be in New York. You can call me or my secretary with any details or questions."

She nodded, not looking up. A shadow crossed her sketch. She looked up, thinking he'd gone, but he stood above her. He roughly pulled her up to him, the pad and pencil falling. His kiss was punishing and desperate, seeking the very core of her. She held on through the clutch of pain, and still, even in her shame, suffered the sting of loss as his lips left hers.

He pulled away and looked at her for a long time. She saw fatigue around his eyes and mouth, and something else. Something that hadn't been in his face before. He turned and left her without a word. He turned left off the stone walkway and was gone.

"Goodbye, Colin," she whispered to the air around her. Then the words, waiting patiently, were said for the first and last time before being washed away by tears.

"I love you."

HE WENT AS FAR as the rocks before he knew he could go no farther. He sat in the silver-green grasses, looking to the water but seeing nothing. If he hadn't loved her, he wouldn't have had to find out. If he hadn't felt the blood running in his veins and his heart beating in his throat, it wouldn't have mattered if the touches and laughter and words on the island were real or further embroidery of an elaborate plan.

Now he knew. Now he knew. And he loved her still.

He was, in the end, his father's son. He felt as if he knew him now, his father, knew him as intimately as the skin stretched tight across his bandy knuckles. He understood now how a man could betray his family, turn his back on everything he'd been taught, risk his very world for one touch of his lover's lips. Passion.

He wondered, when the plane began to plummet, if his father reached for his mistress and smiled, knowing his sweet torture was over.

Colin's shoulders bent like an old man's, then shuddered as a dry sob passed through his body.

"EVERYONE MUST COME as their favorite fantasy. No one gets in without a costume," Aimee said, pouring tea and offering it to Della Stevens.

"But what will you be dressed as?" Cecilia Rathmore asked.

Aimee squeezed a lemon wedge into her Limoges cup. "Why, the biggest fantasy of all...the bride."

Vivian's sniff was audible above the reporters' closed-teeth chuckles. After the *Lifestyle* cover, or, as Vivian had overheard it called among the wait staff, "The Blowfish and The Bluefish," Aimee had been forbidden to continue her courtship of the press. She had responded by inviting columnists and reporters from several of the bigger publications over for tea. Knowing any efforts to censure Aimee now could result in a bigger fiasco than the *Lifestyle* cover, Vivian was reduced to monitoring the affair.

"Come now, Vivian." Aimee turned her attention to her. "You must have a favorite fantasy?"

"If I did," she pronounced in her soft, flat voice, "it'd have nothing to do with dressing up."

"Vivian, you naughty nanny, you. C'mon, there must be someone you'd like to pretend to be? How 'bout Marie Antoinette? Cruella De Vil? Lucrezia Borgia? I could whip you up a stunning sharkskin, off-the-shoulder toga number."

Vivian's distaste was cool and smooth as the linen cheek she saved for select, social kisses. Aimee could smell her signature fragrance in the air.

"It's beyond me why you persist in this nonsense.

Obviously, from the favorable response at the fashion show, your designs show talent. All the outfits you've designed for me have been well received. You may be at the brink of a very bright future."

The others murmured assent. They heard a compliment. Aimee heard Vivian's veiled reminder of their agreement. And exactly as Vivian had planned it, she was forced to publicly acknowledge her benefactress.

"Thank you," she said to the muted sheen of satisfaction in Vivian's eyes.

Still, she knew what Vivian had said was true. The day of the fashion show, her designs had moved down the runway as if not needing the wispy bodies beneath them. They'd pirouetted and pranced, a chorus line of color and cloth. Then, when Vivian had revealed to the ladies who lunched that her own outfit had been designed by Aimee, the orders had started to flow like the champagne cocktails. Of course, after next weekend, Vivian would declare a new opinion regarding Aimee's talents, and the orders would be canceled.

"And Colin will be the other ultimate fantasy?" she heard a reporter ask. "A groom?"

She left her thoughts behind and answered "Yes" amid the knowing twitters of laughter. She looked at Vivian. "The entire wedding will be what it was meant to be—the ultimate fantasy."

AIMEE PAUSED at the ballroom's entrance. The room was draped in gold and trimmed in ivory. A crystal chandelier shattered the sunlight into a thousand rainbow tears. She stood very still, hearing the ghosts—

the high, brittle laughter of women, the lingering tremble of conversation, the clink of ice against glass.

"Imagining the happy day?"

Her head jerked like a fish hooked. Her eyes met Colin's. Today was Friday. He'd returned as he said he would. Tomorrow was their wedding day. She almost stepped toward him, then stopped.

"You're home," she said.

"I'm back," he corrected. His expression was grim, world-weary. His smile was no more than a twist. She thought of another Colin, laughing above her, his chest still damp and heaving. She took a step back.

He looked around the ivory-gold room. "As the blessed event draws near, you must be filled with joy."

She took another step back.

"Where are you going?" He seized her wrist.

She wrenched her arm away, sucking in a gasp of pain as Colin's grip tightened.

"It's too hot in here." She heard the plea in her voice. "Let's go outside. I'll show you the garden tent where the ceremony will take place."

He yanked her arm up, pulling her close. Her head snapped back. Her captive hand clenched, her fingernails piercing her palm. Colin's lips drew back into a thin smile. Coldness cloaked Aimee's heart.

"But you still owe me a dance, remember?" He referred to the fateful night they first met. He dragged her into the center of the room, her high heels clicking against the polished floor. "We'll practice our wedding waltz."

He stopped, looked sharply at her face. Her lips pressed in soundless anger and pain. Sadness, dry as ashes, filled her.

"What's the matter, my love? Prewedding jitters?" He forced her against him. She twisted away, but he held her fast. His arm circled her waist like a vise. Silk met steel.

"Tomorrow we'll marry." He began to turn slowly. "Husband and wife, a sacred bond." His speed increased. "United as one."

They swirled faster and faster. *"Those whom God has joined together, let no man put asunder."* With a sharp contraction, Colin's arm became a band of pain around her waist. Aimee's breath caught in her chest. The band of pain around her heart tightened.

The room twirled around in flashes of ivory and gold and blinding sunlight. She was swimming, spinning in a whirlpool created, controlled by Colin. Her hair whipped back off her face, exposing her neck. She fixed her gaze on the pulse tracing the edge of his jaw and waited for the tempest to subside.

He stopped. She lurched against him, hitting the hard wall of his chest. His arms went slack, steadying her. Everything went still. They had reached the false calm at the center of the storm. He held her for a remorseless minute more, then thrust her away from him.

She staggered backward, her hands clutching at the empty air behind her until she regained her balance.

They stood, once lovers, now wounded.

"Thanks for the dance," he said. He turned and walked with even paces to the door. He didn't look back.

THE PANTOMIME CONTINUED with a short rehearsal that evening, and afterward, a small dinner party. There were chilled oysters, chilled champagne, a roasted rack of lamb and wild mushrooms. Aimee had invited Jack and several of the Portuguese fishermen who'd served as waiters at the fashion show. Their dark complexions were ruddy from the shading of candlelight and the champagne that tasted like flowers. Shawn sat in their midst, exchanging ribald stories and low laughter. Possibly twenty, thirty years from now, his features would slacken and his boyish-beautiful face look incongruous on an old man, but tonight, in the gilded light, he was at the peak of perfection, his only concern champagne and charm.

Vivian was unperturbable, almost amiable, this evening, her ash-blond hair piled high on her head and her cheekbones ivory smooth whenever she smiled. Hugo hadn't been feeling well and had declined to join them. Colin sat in his grandfather's place at the end of the table.

"To the happy day!" Manuel said in heavily accented English as he rose to his feet, his champagne glass high in the air.

Vivian raised her own glass. "To the happy day!"

Others lifted their glasses, then drank. Aimee raised her champagne to her lips, but didn't drink. She saw Colin watching her.

"To the beautiful bride," Shawn toasted.

"Yes, to the bride" was murmured as glasses raised again.

Unsmiling, his face all hollows, Colin lifted his own glass and paid homage to her.

She pushed away from the table. "Excuse me,"

she told the guests. She didn't start to run until she reached the double French doors. She went through them and, kicking off her thin-strapped heels and pulling up the long skirts of the silk slips she'd put on, one after the other, like a child dressing up in mommy's clothes, she ran, wishing she had wings and could fly.

She went to the pebbled beach, the cracked shells piercing her soles and the mist, like morning dew, on her skin. The lights of the houses were behind her, but before her, there were no stars in the sky, and farther out, the blackness of the ocean became the blackness of the night.

She hugged herself, her many colored slips thin sheaths against the night wind. She rubbed her hands up and down, feeling the length of her arms and her bones like stripped twigs. A warm breath feathered against the back of her neck. Her hands stopped their movement.

A jacket slid along her bared shoulders. Fingertips stayed on the curve of her neck, their touch light but firm.

"Nervous?" Colin asked. She could tell by the direction of his voice he was looking out to the ocean.

She was turned around, meeting the eyes dark as the night and the sea. She laid a restraining hand against his chest, her fingers splaying against a web of hard muscle. The skin tightened, the muscle swelled, then slackened against her palm with each of Colin's even breaths.

"Go away," she said, her voice a strangled whisper.

His grip tightened. "Cold feet? Second thoughts?" Contempt wintered his voice.

"This isn't what I wanted." She threw her head back, bold beneath the night's cover. "This isn't how I expected it to be."

His brows arched, the line of his mouth curving without humor. "And how did you expect it to be? Like this?"

Curled with anger, his mouth took hers, his lips hard and cool, devouring. She pressed her hand against his chest. He ignored her protests, his tongue only thrusting deeper, forcing her lips apart wider, plunging deep inside her with driving rhythm.

Her hand went limp, sliding down the relief of his rib cage, settling on the hard edge of his hip. His tongue probed, his lips pressed harder, bruising her mouth. Consciousness drained beneath his brutal, tantalizing touch. She became the blackness of the night and the sea.

"Or did you imagine it like this?" he growled against her parted mouth. His lips turned to velvet. His tongue traced the slack outline of her mouth. Slowly, deliberately, he savored each corner, then lightly drew her bottom lip into his mouth. He tugged gently. His tongue brushed across her opened mouth, drawing desire. Her hands lifted, found his shoulders to steady her. His tongue, warm and moist, delicately tasted and sampled, flitting across the parted hollow of her lips. There was the timelessness of desire around them, binding them. She tried to draw his tongue into her, but it resisted, its tip teasing.

Only when she was pressed up against him, long-ing expressed in the tight, hard tremble of her body, did he enter her open mouth, slowly, tasting of breath and perfumed wine. She tried to drink him, and his tongue retreated to the gap of her lips, then entered her mouth again, carefully, testing, finding the soft insides of her cheeks, the tip of her own tongue. The kiss went on and on, never quickening, until Aimee's head moved with its slow-waltz rhythm. When it ended with a last lingering touch of Colin's lips, she kept her eyes closed, running the tip of her own tongue across her lips, tasting him still.

Then she opened her eyes, and he was waiting, watching her without expression. She laid her palms along the shadows of his face and drew him to her, rubbing her closed eyes against his brow, his hollowed cheeks, the blunt line of his jaw. She closed his eyes with light, christening kisses, then lingered for a moment on those lids, learning the fragile, thin skin covering the darkness below. Her mouth, parted, reverent, skimmed his skin, his shadowed throat, the silken cloth of his shirt. When she sought his mouth, his lips were already open. Her tongue tasted the smooth edge of his teeth. Her lips kissed his, her mouth silently singing what she'd never dare to say aloud.

She stepped back, her hands still framing Colin's face. There, reflected in the smoky softness of his opened eyes, revealed in the soundless breath parting his lips, Aimee saw the same unspeakable emotion.

"That is how I imagined it," she said.

Chapter Fourteen

Aimee laid the gown out across the bed. Its satin skirt was full, its overlay of tulle covered with glass beads that caught at the sun. Its top was sleeveless and sheer, fastened by a row of tiny, glass-bead buttons down its back. It was a fairy-tale dress, she'd thought, when she'd designed it. It deserved a happy ending.

She sat down on the corner of the bed, touching the dress's smooth satin, delicate tulle. She felt the material slide through her fingers.

There would be no happy endings for this gown or its wearer.

She stood and headed for the bath. It was time to get ready for her wedding day.

COLIN COULDN'T HELP IT. He had to laugh. The tented tennis court looked wilder than a Christian Lacroix spring showing. Inside its voile-lined walls, guests sat in frothy crinolines and towering Louis XIV powdered wigs. There were flamboyant capes and bullfighter jackets and Glinda, the Good Witch. There were pirate eye patches and Rhett Butler mustaches and one amazing resemblance to a famous politician until Colin realized it was the real person. One of the ushers wore dreadlocks, and some of the country's wealthiest and powerful men were in drag. Peacocks paraded up and down the aisles and around the grounds. A one-man band played ''Muskrat Love.''

Aimee would love this, Colin thought. But would she be here to see it? She'd said yes to his proposal, but she'd also said yes to Vivian. Had she successfully hedged her bets? Had he unwittingly played right into her hands?

She could be on her way now to meet Vivian and Shawn at the town hall or another appointed place of rendezvous where a justice of the peace awaited them. Or she could be upstairs, dressing, dotting her pulse points with French perfume, combing up her long hair, coloring her mouth, readying to become his bride. Or she could already be here, watching him from behind one of the many feathered and sequined half masks. He didn't know.

And he didn't know what he wanted more: for her to show up or not to show up. Did it matter? Either way, whether she married Shawn or himself, she'd fulfilled her expectations...and his.

Still, he wanted her like no other. He'd tried to despise her, but found only desire. He could only despise himself, his weakness.

A woman dressed in a nurse's uniform appeared from between the voile curtains and gestured to him. At first he thought it was one of the costumed guests waving hello. Then he realized it was Hugo's day nurse.

He hurried to meet her. "Has something happened? Is Hugo okay?"

"He's as well as can be expected," she answered, "but he's asked to see you."

Colin rushed to the house. He found Hugo in the study, seated in a burgundy leather chair, his skin pallid and pleated. But the whites of his eyes were clear, almost bright.

"You're a lucky man today, Colin," his grandfather said.

"That would be the general opinion," he answered, neither confirming nor denying.

Hugo picked up a large FedEx envelope from his lap and offered it to him. "I've an early wedding present for you. Read this."

Colin took the envelope and slid out the papers inside it. He scanned the cover page and looked questioningly at his grandfather.

"Read it," Hugo urged impatiently.

He did as he was told, and when he finished he looked up at the old man.

Hugo smiled. "Your beloved bride obviously didn't read Shakespeare. If she had, she would've learned it takes more than a name to give a rose its sweet smell."

Colin's grip tightened on the report detailing Aimee's impoverished childhood in Providence, her mother's drug addiction and death at a young age, Aimee's subsequent foster care until she reached legal age. At that time she'd changed her name and come to Newport.

He looked down at the neatly typed words once more. Had she changed her name, hoping to forge a new future, trying to change the past? Had she been afraid she'd never be more than her mother's daughter? As afraid as he'd been of never being more than his father's son?

He bowed his head. If so, the anger she'd expressed about Vivian's offer wouldn't have been a ploy. It would've been real. As real and frightening as the emotion he felt for her.

"Imagine, the girl almost had her hooks—lock, stock and barrel—into the Tremont family name and fortune."

"Thank you, Hugo." Colin stood up.

"I knew you'd thank me," the old man said. "I'll have James explain to our guests the wedding is off."

"The wedding's not off," Colin said, walking to the door.

"The wedding's not off?" Hugo called after him. "Have you taken leave of your senses? She's a whore's daughter."

Colin stopped at the doorway. He turned around, meeting his grandfather's indignant expression. "And I'm a whore's son."

Color rose in the old man's sallow skin.

"Look at me, Hugo. Isn't that what you see?" Colin demanded. "Isn't that all you've ever seen?"

Bones rose in the old man's hands as he grasped the chair's smooth arms. "I couldn't save my son." He held Colin in his gaze. "But I saved you. I gave you everything."

Everything he could afford to, Colin thought. The anger, the pain he'd thought conquered came again, stronger, assailing.

Hugo pulled himself forward, his hands gripping the leather arms embracing him. "I paid for the mistakes of your father."

"No." One small word…and the end was begun. Colin felt his body steel, fighting the fear, the pain. He heard his voice, hollow but hard.

"I paid for the mistakes of my father."

He struggled to keep his body tall, strong, even as his muscles seemed to slacken. He'd tried his whole life to gain others' acceptance, love. It'd only come once.

Aimee.

She'd given him herself. He'd offered her a clothing line. His anger singed, grayed with shame.

It'd been easier to doubt her than to love her. It'd been easier to protect himself by nurturing his suspicions.

All she'd given him was the one thing he desired the most.

All he'd given her was the one thing she despised the most.

He had to find her. He had to tell her everything— his fear, his foolishness, his hope for her forgiveness. It wasn't too late. *Please,* he pleaded as he started to leave, *don't make it too late.*

"If you marry her, you won't get a cent," Hugo decreed.

Colin turned and faced his grandfather. "If I marry her, if she'll have me—" he sent a prayer to heaven above "—I'll have everything I need."

"She's not one of us," Hugo called out to him.

"No, she's a Rose," Colin said. "Among the

thorns.'' He turned his back to the dying man and left.

VIVIAN AND SHAWN were waiting for Aimee outside city hall. As she walked toward them, Vivian's thinly-elegant brows arched.

"Was all this necessary?" she asked, looking Aimee up and down.

Aimee straightened her body resplendent in satin and tulle. She smoothed her hands across the fabric. "My shroud's at the cleaners."

Vivian made a clicking noise with her tongue.

"You look beyond beautiful, Aimee," Shawn complimented.

"Let's go," Vivian interrupted crisply. "We're already late." She sailed past them and through the entrance doors.

Aimee looked at Shawn. "And I was worried she'd get all sentimental on us."

He laughed his lovely laugh. "Don't worry about Mother. You look gorgeous."

She smiled her thanks and started toward the doors, but Shawn took her hand, stopping her.

She looked at him curiously.

"I like you, Aimee…I want you to be happy."

"I will be, Shawn. And you'll be, too."

"So you're sure about this?"

She nodded. "I've never been more sure about anything in my life."

He squeezed her hand, and they started to walk toward the building. "Still, I don't imagine this is how you pictured the 'big' day?"

She smiled up at him. She felt the deep, bittersweet pain in her breast. "It's exactly how I pictured it."

Inside, Vivian was waiting for them at the bottom of the staircase. "You've got the license, right?" she asked Shawn.

"That's the third time you've asked me that," he chided.

Aimee knew, however, there was a much more important piece of paper needed before the ceremony could begin. She laid a hand on Shawn's arm. "Could you give Vivian and me a minute?"

He looked at her. "You two aren't going to tie tin cans on the Fiat, are you?"

She returned his smile. "Go on ahead. We'll be right up."

She waited until Shawn reached the second landing, then turned to Vivian. "Do you have it?" she asked.

Vivian looked down the length of her long, thin nose. "Of course I have it."

"Give it to me." Aimee held out her hand.

Vivian lifted an arched brow. "Here? Right now?"

"Give it to me now or I'm out that door and saying 'I do' to Colin before you can say 'Disinherited.'"

Vivian unsnapped the interlinked *C* clasp on her quilted leather bag, her pale eyes like glass. "I'll be ecstatic when this is all over."

"For once you and I agree on something, Viv." Aimee took the thin slip of paper handed her and examined it. With a smile, she hitched up her satin slip and tucked the paper into her garter. She wiggled so the skirt fell back into place, then straightened her bodice.

"Are you through?" Vivian asked, her thin lips barely moving.

"Come on, Viv." Aimee linked her arm through the other woman's as they started up the stairs. "Just think, if all goes as planned, soon everyone will be calling you 'Grandma.'"

All the color left Vivian's face.

Shawn was chatting with the judge when the women arrived.

"I thought you ran out on me," he teased.

"I tried, but Vivian's quicker. This lady has a mean long jump."

Vivian held her hand out to the judge. "The sooner we begin, the better."

"Certainly. Let me just buzz my secretary to serve as the other witness. We'll put the groom here and the bride beside him."

A stout woman from the reception area came in.

"Edith, you aren't going to cry, are you?" the judge asked.

The ample secretary shook her gray, tightly permed crown. She looked at Aimee, pulled a tissue from the rolled cuff of her sleeve, blew into it loudly, then waved at the judge to begin.

The judge cleared his throat. "We've gathered here today to witness the union of…"

They're only words, Aimee thought. Still she couldn't help but think of another man who waited for her, ready to repeat the same words—words of hope and promise and pledge, words of young girls' dreams and old women's remembrances. But, said there or said here, they wouldn't be words of love. They would be only words.

"Do you, Aimee Rose, take this man, Shawn Leland Tremont, to have and to hold from this day forward, for better or for worse, for richer, for poorer, in sickness and in health, to love and to cherish until death do you part?"

The room was silent, waiting for her answer. Aimee looked up at Shawn's fair face. "I don't."

"What?" Vivian exploded. Shawn looked at Aimee with confusion and question.

"You don't?" the judge exclaimed.

Aimee reached into her bosom.

"Good God!" Vivian sputtered.

From her bodice, Aimee pulled out a small folded square of paper and handed it to Shawn.

"This is for you," she said.

Shawn unfolded the piece of paper. He let out a low whistle, then looked at Aimee. "I don't understand."

"It's a wedding present."

"But you don't want to marry me?"

She laid a hand on his forearm. "No, but some day, some girl will, and you'll want to marry her. It's a present for that wedding—a wedding based on love, not money."

Shawn leaned down and softly kissed Aimee's cheek. "Thank you. At this moment, you're the girl of my dreams," he whispered.

"Go on, get out of here, before I change my mind," she teased.

"Shawn! Shawn!" Vivian's voice rose, almost approached a yell as her son walked out of the office.

"What've you done? Where's he going?" she demanded of Aimee as the door closed.

"I imagine he's going to the bank," Aimee calmly replied.

"What've you done?" Vivian took a step toward her.

"I wrote him a check for the exact amount that was transferred into my account this morning."

Vivian's face blanched, and for a moment her body wavered. "All of it?"

Aimee nodded.

"Vivian, can I get you a chair? A glass of water?" the judge offered.

She turned to him with her white-teeth smile. "Perhaps a moment alone here with Aimee. Thank you."

She waited until the door closed behind the judge and his secretary.

"You little fool." She turned on Aimee. "You never had any intention of marrying Shawn at all, did you?"

"Marriage is for love, Vivian, not for money."

"Then why did you say yes?"

"I wanted to prove something to you. I wanted to prove something to myself. Now I understand why some people can't resist temptation. And I learned how hard it is to say no to something you want more than anything else in the world." Aimee knew Vivian would think she was referring to the wealth and her rising reputation in the fashion industry. Only Aimee knew she wasn't thinking of those things at all.

Vivian eyed her. "You gave it all up—the money, the status, the success?"

"I can't say it wasn't fun while it lasted."

"Why?" Vivian had to ask again.

"The price was too high."

The other woman shook her head. "That's why there's so many more poor people and so few really rich."

"Why?" Aimee had to ask.

"Scruples." Vivian cursed.

Aimee burst out laughing. "Vivian, you are the genuine article."

"Go on." Vivian waved her hands, dismissing her. "Go back to your little apartment and your little life."

Aimee started toward the door.

"I might've lost," Vivian said behind her, "but you didn't win."

Aimee reached for the door handle, the pain making her suddenly unsteady on her feet. "I know."

COLIN RAN UP the stairs and down the hall to Aimee's bedroom. The door was open, the room neat. He didn't see any of her things. Where was she?

He started to leave when he heard the sound of running water from behind the closed bathroom door. She was still here. She was getting ready. Relief welled within him.

He walked over to the closed door and tapped lightly. "I know this is a hell of a time to be telling you this. I should've told you before, but...I love you."

The bathroom door swung open. Behind it stood

James, a toilet bowl brush in his hand. "Thank you, sir. I've grown quite fond of you also."

Colin clasped him by the shoulders. "Where is she?"

"Miss Aimee had her things packed and sent to her apartment yesterday. Although Miss Aimee isn't one for convention, I assumed she'd chosen to get ready in her apartment so the groom wouldn't see the bride before the wedding. I was quite surprised when she came down to breakfast this morning. She didn't eat a thing though."

"When's the last time you saw her?" Colin demanded.

"Shortly after breakfast. She said she came to say goodbye to me. Kissed me on the cheek." The old man smiled.

"Say goodbye?" Colin asked.

"Yes, sir. She looked beautiful, too. More like a sugar plum fairy than a bride."

"She had her wedding dress on?"

James nodded. "Yes, sir."

Colin hurried out of the room and down the stairs to the back of the house. He headed toward the tent where they were to take their vows. She was in there, he told himself with each quick step he took. She was probably wondering right now where he was.

He walked into the tent. The murmur of low voices stopped. Heads turned his way. He looked up the aisle, to the sides, in between the rows of costumed and feathered spectators. He didn't see her.

If she wasn't here, where was she? Where else would she go in a wedding dress? She wouldn't...she couldn't…he couldn't even allow the alternative thought to form in his head.

He saw Hugo at the tent's entrance. Vivian was beside him, but he didn't see Aimee…or Shawn. He walked down the aisle toward them. If his worst fear was true, if Aimee had married Shawn, it'd be his fault. He'd been too proud, too arrogant, too afraid to tell her his true feelings. Instead he'd insulted her, degraded her, led her to think she was nothing more than what she feared most.

"I can't find her," he said when he reached his grandfather. He looked at Vivian. "She's gone."

"Consider yourself lucky, my boy. I meant what I said inside. If you'd married that woman, you'd find yourself cut out of the will faster than a Whitney racehorse."

Colin was still looking at Vivian, waiting for her reaction.

"What're you talking about, Hugo?" she said, a flush spreading across her face.

It was true, Colin thought. Pain filled the empty part of him that'd once been his heart. Aimee had married Shawn.

"That girl was born one step away from the gutter. She changed her name to hide her past, but I had an investigator check out her family. Her mother was a prostitute. Heaven knows who her father was. If Colin insisted on marrying this woman, I'd have no choice but to cut him out of the will."

Colin looked up at Vivian, expecting anger, distress, infuriation. She was smiling. Smiling, hell, she was laughing. A great, big, undignified laugh that caused the peacocks to stop their promenade and swivel their elegant heads to her.

Her carefully orchestrated plan just blew up in her face, and she was laughing? Was it hysteria, the beginning stages of shock? Yet her laughter didn't sound maniacal. It sounded relieved.

"Vivian," he said. "Where's Shawn?"

"Shawn?" Vivian wiped at her eyes. "Probably celebrating." Her laughter started once more.

"Celebrating? Why would he be celebrating?"

"He came into a little money. A million dollars."

"A million dollars?" Hugo exclaimed. "Who'd give him that kind of money?"

Vivian's laughter started once more. "A girl from the gutter," she said between laughing breaths.

"Where is she? Where's Aimee?" Colin grabbed Vivian by the shoulders.

She shrugged off his hold. "Probably in some godforsaken two-room apartment with her honor intact."

Colin turned and faced the guests. "Don't anyone leave." He pointed a finger at the justice of the peace seated up front. "Especially you. I'm getting married today."

"Are you mad? You marry that woman, and you'll have nothing," Hugo warned.

"No." Colin's single syllable of defiance rang through the tent. He looked down at his grandfather. "I'll marry that woman, and I'll have everything."

HE FOUND HER heading toward the wharves. She seemed to be floating in a gossamer cloud, an angel oblivious to the mere mortals who stopped and turned when she passed.

He pulled over and parked. "Aimee," he called. He saw her misstep, stop, then continue. He was running to her now. As he got close, he saw the shimmer of thousands of rainbows caught in her dress. When he reached her and stood before her, he saw the shimmer of tears across her face.

"Oh, no, no. Don't cry. You told me you wouldn't cry on our wedding day." He raised his hand to touch her cheek, her tears. She turned her face away. His hand stopped. Afraid.

"Aimee," he whispered, he called.

He had to tell her everything: what a fool he'd been; how his feelings for her were unlike any others, existing beyond conscious thought, rising from the part of him that was simple, complex, most passionate, most frightened. Their power, their beauty scared him, awed him. His fear had fought them, whispering words of mistrust, suspicion, narrowing his perception, seeking to keep him safe from pain—a pain manufactured in his mind.

He was hers, had always been hers. That was everything, the beginning, the end.

He had to tell her all these things. And he did with three words.

"I love you." He took a breath and his world expanded.

"I love you."

She was looking at him now, cheeks glassy with tears.

"And it scares the hell out of me."

Her hand lifted slightly. Her fingers were trembling. She didn't seem aware of it. All her focus, her question, was within her eyes.

"So I fought it, feeding my suspicions, forcing myself to believe what you aren't. You gave me your heart, I responded with a vile offer. Forgive me."

Her hand lifted a little higher. Her eyes watched him.

"Hugo has decided he disapproves of our marriage and will disinherit me if it proceeds. Did he expect me to hesitate, to sacrifice my heart, my happiness for silver? Then I remembered my own offer to you. I'm ashamed."

She didn't speak nor move, her thoughts within her.

"I offer you only myself now. I give you everything I am. I'm yours."

He'd never felt the fear so strong. It rode in his blood, prickled his skin, soured his saliva. If he lost her now, he lost everything.

Her hand, shaking, slowly rose. Her fingertips met his in the most fragile of touches, no more than a wing's tremor. Her eyes were steady and wondrous.

"You are all I ever wanted."

Her fingers curled, fell between his. He pulled her into his arms, his smiling mouth coming down on hers. The kiss became laughter and lightness. Their bodies met in a press of tulle and satin. Her heart, beaded and rainbowed, was his.

His lips left hers only long enough to beg, "Marry me."

There was no more than a whisper. "Yes."

Their lips met once more.

And all the riches in the world were theirs.

**Starting December 1999,
a brand-new series about
fatherhood from**

Three charming stories
about dads and kids...
and the women who
make their families
complete!

Available December 1999
FAMILY TO BE (#805)
by Linda Cajio

Available January 2000
A PREGNANCY AND A PROPOSAL (#809)
by Mindy Neff

Available February 2000
FOUR REASONS FOR FATHERHOOD (#813)
by Muriel Jensen

Available at your favorite retail outlet.

Visit us at: www.romance.net

HARDC

If you enjoyed what you just read,
then we've got an offer you can't resist!

Take 2 bestselling love stories FREE!

Plus get a FREE surprise gift!

Clip this page and mail it to Harlequin Reader Service®

IN U.S.A.	IN CANADA
3010 Walden Ave.	P.O. Box 609
P.O. Box 1867	Fort Erie, Ontario
Buffalo, N.Y. 14240-1867	L2A 5X3

YES! Please send me 2 free Harlequin American Romance® novels and my free surprise gift. Then send me 4 brand-new novels every month, which I will receive months before they're available in stores. In the U.S.A., bill me at the bargain price of $3.34 plus 25¢ delivery per book and applicable sales tax, if any*. In Canada, bill me at the bargain price of $3.71 plus 25¢ delivery per book and applicable taxes**. That's the complete price and a savings of over 10% off the cover prices—what a great deal! I understand that accepting the 2 free books and gift places me under no obligation ever to buy any books. I can always return a shipment and cancel at any time. Even if I never buy another book from Harlequin, the 2 free books and gift are mine to keep forever. So why not take us up on our invitation. You'll be glad you did!

154 HEN CNEX
354 HEN CNEY

Name _____ (PLEASE PRINT)

Address _____ Apt.#

City _____ State/Prov. _____ Zip/Postal Code

* Terms and prices subject to change without notice. Sales tax applicable in N.Y.
** Canadian residents will be charged applicable provincial taxes and GST.
All orders subject to approval. Offer limited to one per household.
® are registered trademarks of Harlequin Enterprises Limited.

AMER99 ©1998 Harlequin Enterprises Limited

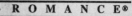
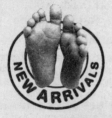

3 Stories of Holiday Romance from three
bestselling Harlequin® authors

Valentine Babies
by
ANNE STUART

TARA TAYLOR QUINN

JULE McBRIDE

Goddess in Waiting by Anne Stuart
Edward walks into Marika's funky maternity shop to pick
up some things for his sister. He doesn't expect to assist
in the delivery of a baby and fall for outrageous Marika.

Gabe's Special Delivery by Tara Taylor Quinn
On February 14, Gabe Stone finds a living, breathing
valentine on his doorstep—his daughter. Her mother
has given Gabe four hours to adjust to fatherhood,
resolve custody and win back his ex-wife?

My Man Valentine by Jule McBride
Everyone knows Eloise Hunter and C. D. Valentine
are in love. Except Eloise and C. D. Then, one of
Eloise's baby-sitting clients leaves her with a baby to
mind, and C. D. swings into protector mode.

VALENTINE BABIES
On sale January 2000 at your favorite retail outlet.

HARLEQUIN®
Makes any time special ™

Visit us at www.romance.net